KIKA AND SNIFF

Printed in the United States of America

First Printing, 2019
ISBN: 9781090530646

Library of Congress Control Number:
 2019900639

Cover Design:
Illustrations: Brandon McKinney

Book Interior and Production:
LuckyCinda
www.luckycinda.com

Distributed by Ingram:
One Ingram Blvd., La Vergne, TN 37086
615.793.5000

KIKA AND SNIFF

Adventure in the Belowlands

Kat Sawyer

Illustrations by Brandon McKinney

To you who are waiting for your Adventure to begin.

CHAPTER 1

There – through the cattails – she saw it – a headless dog.

She crept closer. The creature, buried shoulder-deep in a gopher hole, dug with determination, his big brown bottom wiggling, dirt flying all over the place.

The girl giggled. At the sound of her voice, the dog backed out. They gazed into each other's eyes. So, okay, not to get all mushy and stuff, but from that moment, Snifferton Woolypads and Catalina "Kika" Lucia Jones knew they would be best budds forever.

Kika guessed he was part Lab, part Pit, and part something else – a scrawny brown New Mexico dog with an amazing nose, a curious nature, and a passion for excavation. He ferreted out rabbits, packrats, greasy taco wrappers, and gophers, digging so much that his paw pads were scratchy as scrubby sponges.

Kika took great care of her new pal, fattening up his skinny bones and nursing his sore neck, red and raw from where the hair had been rubbed off. It looked like he'd escaped from someone who kept him chained. He's a happy pup now, though.

Kika thinks about these things as she fixes breakfasts for the two of them. Juggling the brimming bowls, she elbows out the screen door and tiptoes onto the shady *portal*, being super quiet, because this is her mother's only morning to sleep in.

Where is that dog? thinks Kika.

She sets down her cereal and shuffles out the open gate. Picking up a stone, she clinks the side of the metal dog dish. No Snifferton.

He's probably adventuring somewhere. No use waiting out here for a billion years, though.

Kika leaves his kibble, ambles back onto the porch, and plops down in the rickety bent-willow rocker. Her neon-pink T-shirt feels too hot for the day and her apple-green shorts, too stupid. She fishes a Cheerio out of her bowl and looks through it like a telescope. Gazing down at her bare feet, she wishes they weren't so huge. *They look gigantic – like flippers. Ick.* She picks at the polish on her toenails. *Tangerine Sky? Dumb name.*

Kika lugs her backpack over and pulls out her sketchbook. She thumbs through it, and stops at the design for her *quinceañeara* outfit – a sparkly white gown, tiara and high heels. Kika sighs. *Four more years before I'm ever going to wear this.* She flips the book closed. Even drawing doesn't interest her this morning. She wedges the sketches back into her pack next to a sweatshirt, three crumpled spelling tests, a flashlight, half-full water bottle, dog treats, cell with zero charge, and one petrified cube of Dubble Bubble.

I really should clean this thing out. But not now. I'm way too busy being bored. Kika zips up the bag and revisits her cereal.

Another sigh. Maybe today won't be such a snore.

Kika's mother promised to take her to Rudy's Grill for green chili cheeseburgers and shakes, then shopping for back-to-school stuff. She'll have Mami all to herself and they won't need to squeeze their time together between other things. These outings don't happen very often because Mami is extremely busy with work at the hospital and taking care of Abuelita, Kika's grandmother. Mami isn't a rock star mom, but she is pretty neat, except for being distracted a little and worried a lot. Kika knows that a divorced parent's job is intense so she tries to be quiet and helpful and good and not stress her mother out too much. She just wishes Mami was happier.

Kika is looking forward to finding some great clothes today and decent-looking shoes that actually fit her giant boats. Looking cute is super important on the "First Day," especially this first day, because Kika is in sixth, which means MIDDLE SCHOOL. *There'll be so many other kids and so much more homework. What if I can't remember where all my classes are? What if I forget the combination to my locker? What if I don't have the same lunch period as Patricia?* Patricia is Kika's best, and, well, only friend.

The good news? Kika's not a little elementary baby anymore. She hopes that in middle school she won't feel like a dork and JP will talk to her for once.

She also wonders why she chopped her hair so short that she looks like a guy.

Answer? Because, number one, Judi, the most popular girl in fifth, cut hers and she looks awesome. Number two, all of Kika's favorite celebs have pixies, and, number three, Mami told her that short hair is easier for summer and swimming. *But,* thinks Kika wistfully, *Judi's ears don't stick out, I'm not a celebrity, and most of the year isn't summer.*

Oh, well. Maybe if I plaster my bangs down with gel, I won't look so hideous.

On a more positive note, Kika doesn't totally hate her appearance. She likes her toasty skin, the color of *café con leche*, her brownish-greenish eyes flecked with gold, her ... well, that's about it.

Kika yawns a third time and spoons into her Cheerios. She likes the way they bob in the warmish milk – little life preservers in a white sea. *I wish I was floating in the ocean right now.*

Anywhere but here. Someone please save me from this boredommm!

Boogers, boogers, boogers!! What a weird word.

Kika slurps up the last of her breakfast and thinks about how to fill the long hours ahead. As her toes push the rocker, it makes a croaking noise that sounds like *waiting, waiting, waiting.*

Why am I always waiting for some thing or another?
I wait for friends, the bus, my dog, my grandma and my mother.
Okay, 'cause I'm a scaredy-pants. I've never been that bold.
It seems I'm always waiting to be asked or to be told.
I wait all year for school to end and have vacation fun.
What do I do? I wait. I wait for summer to be done!
But I can't wait to learn to drive and finally be a TEEN –

to stay up after twelve and dye my brown
hair pink or green!
Make-up, boyfriends, earning my own
money will be great,
but, sigh, I'm just eleven, so guess I'll have
to wait.
Boogers.

C H A P T E R 2

BAM! The screen door slams shut.

Shoot shoot shoot!

Kika carefully sets her empty cereal bowl in the kitchen sink and listens for bed squeaks and floor creaks and waking-up rustlings from her mother's room.

What was that?

Kika holds her breath.

Whew. Guess it wasn't her. Close one.

She leaves this note on the table:

Dear Mami,
Looking for Sniff. Be back soon.
Love, Kika

Kika figures that looking for Sniff is prefer-able to sitting around the house rotting. Reaching under a chair, she retrieves her favorite thongs, the fancy ones with fake crystals stuck onto the straps. She eases open the door and scoots out. Grabbing her backpack, she scuffs into the early pearly morning.

Kika's snug adobe home with its blue front door glows pink. Autumn is on the breeze. The last cicadas click like castanets in the cottonwood trees. Fading hollyhocks droop their pretty pale heads – not that Kika notices any of this because her mind is whirring like a hamster on a wheel. *Strawberry shake today or vanilla? I hope the ants don't find Sniff's chow. Maybe vanilla. I should have brought it back into the kitchen. No, strawberry. I wonder what dog food tastes like ...*

Lost in space, Kika heads toward the *acequia* – a shallow water channel that runs through the fields. Sniff likes to hang out around there. When it's hot, he digs himself a snooze-zone and every day burrows deeper to expose the cooler dirt underneath.

Shuffling along, Kika's feet kick up feathery dust devils around her ankles.

Weird, she thinks. *Why do my flip-flops sound so loud?*

The insects hush.

Magpies quit their heckling.

Not even a grumble from Mr. Romero's tractor disturbs the quiet September air.

Strangely quiet – like morning holding its breath.

A muted bark unsettles the stillness. *Sniff?*

It stops.

"Snifferton!" Kika calls. She hears it again, closer this time, but still muffled. *How can that be?* Snifferton's bark is coming from *under the ground.*

On hands and knees, Kika presses her ear to the earth. She hears a whimper, definitely beneath her. Dashing to his digging spot, she stares in disbelief at a dark cavity puncturing the ground.

Kika's heart hammers as she kneels down and peers into the crumbling blackness. The hole is low and cramped and spooky. She sits back on her heels. *Okay. Okay. I don't have to go in there. I can just wait up here for him to find his way out. But what if he's trapped? Maybe I should get help. But, if he isn't trapped, he won't be able to follow the sound of my voice.*

Kika cups her hands around her mouth and shouts, "Sniff! Snifferton! Come, boy!"

No answer.

"I have treats!"

Silence.

"Snifferton," she cries. "Please come! Please! I'm scared!"

The earth shivers. Uh-oh.

Kika has a sinking feeling. She scrabbles to get out but the opening is collapsing fast. With a rumble and a shudder the land gives way, taking Kika and the backpack with it. Her fingernails tear at the shifting sand. Faster and deeper and faster and deeper she slides. A scream catches in her throat, as she slips quietly into the hungry belly of the cold, dark, earth.

I'm going to die!

CHAPTER 3

Kika doesn't die. Lucky for Kika – except that she's buried up to her ribs in a gigantic pile of moving dirt – in darkness as black as a night without stars … or a moon … with your eyes closed.

"Help!" she cries. "Heeellllppppp!"

Nothing. Nothing and more nothing.

Boosting up with her arms is impossible because her legs are pinned down tight. "Oh no! No, no, no!" she wails. A wave of panic washes over Kika and her rigid body goes limp.

An eternity later (or a couple of minutes), she

feels nudging at her shoulders. Her heart bounces. A powerful force grabs her pack and pulls hard. Kika backpedals out and crawls to more stable ground. A hot, stinky pant puffs in her face.

"Sniff?" she whimpers.

"Mrf."

"Sniff! I found you!"

"More like I found you," he corrects, shaking the dust out of his pelt. "Are you okay?"

"I … I think so … wait … you can … talk?"

"Yes I can."

"Oh, wow!" she gasps, "You can talk now."

"I could always talk. You just couldn't hear."

"Oh. Oh. Well – wow." Kika loses it again. "Thank you for saving me! Thank you, thank you, thank you. I love you Snifferton." She hugs her big friend tight and kisses the top of his head. Her lips taste like dirt.

"All right. All right, Kika. Simmer down." Regaining his dignity, the dog continues, "I believe that when I return to the surface, I will pursue a career in Search and Rescue. Must be the Retriever in me."

This conversation seems bizarre yet somehow quite natural to Kika. She's accustomed to talking to her dog, but for him to answer is astonishing and really neat.

With some effort, she pushes herself up to a crouch. Her legs feel like Silly String. Miraculously, the flip-flops still cling to her feet. *It's hard to move around in this tight little spot.*

She and Sniff are hemmed in by a bank of shifting soil – if you could see it, but you can't because it's dark. Kika wiggles her backpack free, finds the flashlight, and switches it on. "Look Sniff look!" she cries in wonder. "Everything's so brown!"

"Yes, Kika, it is," replies the dog noting a narrow tunnel nearby. Glancing up at the scary brown mountain that's sliding faster now, he continues, "I think it would be wise to, uh ... leave." He bolts. Kika scrambles.

BWISHHH!

Crashing down behind them, an avalanche of earth sends them racing to outrun it. A monster dust cloud billows forward, and then all goes still.

The two slow to a walk and stop.

Looking back, Kika's flashlight beam trembles as, through the settling silt, they see a mondo wall of earth.

"Do you think it's over?" coughs Kika.

"I believe so," pants Sniff, "at least for now, and now I believe I deserve a treat."

"Oh, of course you do. Without you, Snifferton, we …"

"*Alan.*"

"What?"

"I prefer *Alan.*"

"*Alan?*"

"Yes. That is my name."

"But, we call you Sniff."

"I realize this, but I have always referred to myself as *Alan.*"

Kika had never given any thought to what animals call themselves. A pet iguana might be named Inca, but he knows himself as Carl. Birds in the trees may identify each other by interesting and exotic names like Tweeteetsi or Cawcawzio or Chipp.

"Okaaay – um – Alan," begins Kika, "but if I accidently call you *Sniff,* you won't get all mad, will you?"

"I don't know," he sighs. "Treat, please."

Kika props up the flashlight and pulls a biscuit out of her backpack. Sniff – Alan – receives it with nobility and a soft mouth. Kika takes a gulp of water from her bottle and pours a dribble into her palm. The dog laps delicately.

"So, Alan," starts Kika, "how did you find me?"

"I'm a dog. I sniffed."

"Right. Of course. Duh."

She pulls on her sweatshirt. "It's kind of cold down here."

"Fifty-six degrees Fahrenheit at all times," he states matter-of-factly.

"How did you know that?"

"I read."

Whoa.

Fearing another landslide, Sniff stands.

"Let's move," he says, trotting off – nose to the ground – down the tunnel.

Grabbing her stuff, Kika cries, "Sniff! Where are you going?"

"Forward."

CHAPTER 4

Kika's flashlight casts ghostly shadows along the passageway. She marvels at the silence. Fossils, stones, and boulders bulge from the tunnel walls. Tangles of tree roots snake around them. It smells musty and moist – like Abuelita's cellar. When the prickly feet of giant antler-horned beetles scuttle across Kika's bare toes, she flinches. Chilly whiffs of air weave around her ankles like hungry cats begging for supper. Out of trickling water seeps, blood-red worms poke their shiny heads and sway together like dancers under the sea. It's all so wondrous, mysterious, dusty.

Kika sneezes. "Sniff? Alan. Wait. Check these out."

Her beam reveals primitive symbols and figures scratched into the walls. "This one looks like a rabbit," she says, "or a mole or something, and here's a flying saucer, and a rainbow maybe, and way over here, someone wrote, 'Trolls Rule'. What do you think these are?"

"Petroglyphs," replies Sniff. "Or possibly runes."

Again, *whoa*.

"And, look at this," she says illuminating a carved slab of rock that reads:

WHILE YOU'RE HERE, BE SURE TO VISIT THE WORLD-FAMOUS UNDERGROUND FARMERS MARKET – EVERYTHING DIRT CHEAP! EXIT AHEAD.

Sniff's ears perk. His body freezes and his tail stiffens. His nose quivers.

"What is it, Sniff? I mean Al …"

"Fine. *Sniff* is fine. Whatever. Pay attention. I'm pointing here."

"What is it?"

"Shhh. The air has turned gopherish."

They hear scuffing, then a gravelly voice echoes through the tunnel. "Turn off that stinkin' light!"

"Uhh," says Kika, fumbling for the switch.

"Cut it!"

Everything goes to pitch. A tiny glowing bluish ball hovering three feet off the ground approaches.

"*Rrrrrr*," warns Sniff.

"What the heck …" comes the voice. "How did you two get here – and what do you want?"

Kika gulps, "Umm … horriblecave-in-togetout?"

"Spaces, Pleeeease!"

"The ground collapsed?" she loudly replies, slowly speaking each word. "We got trapped? We would very much like to find our way out and go home?"

"Why do you talk like that?" asks the voice, "And why are you looking at me like I'm an alien life form? And why do you answer questions with questions?"

"I don't know?"

"Oh boy. Questions don't answer questions. But, whatev. Okay. So, first of all – wait … you don't have glow-holes, do you?"

"What?" asks Kika.

"Glow-holes. You got 'em or not?"

"Umm. No? I mean, no. I mean I'm not really sure."

"You're not sure," it grumbles. "Perfect."

A little body materializes out of the darkness, the weird light beaming from its forehead. The creature's pale skin glimmers with downy fuzz. Two sizeable front teeth hanging over his bottom lip give him a slight lisp when he speaks – or – *th-peakths*. The being's rough hands sprout long orange fingernails, and his hair is a tragic attempt at twisting dreads. He bobs his head and sashays forward to a rhythm only he can hear.

"Here," he says reaching into a small satchel.

"Take these."

He holds out headbands made of intricately woven roots. A ball of gleaming rock is set into each one. Kika takes them and looks up blankly. "Um … how do I …"

"Oh, for Petey's sake," he grouses. "I'll put 'em on for ya." He fits the strange headlamp against Kika's brow and slips the other over Sniff's head. "Careful!" yelps the dog. "Neck issues."

"Got it," says the creature gently adjusting the strap.

The tiny stones cast a surprising amount of light. For several minutes, the three simply stare at each other. Sniff sneaks around to the little guy's backside and begins to …

"Sniff!" scolds Kika. "Seriously?"

"My bad."

"Try not to be such a *dog*," she whispers.

The being's black-olive eyes pop behind his glasses. "Dog?" he squeaks. "Did you say D-O-G dog? Oh boy. Oh boy. Have I ever heard about Dogs! The Uptops freak us out with stories about 'em. Gotta warn the others!" He scurries back down the tunnel.

"No. Wait. Wait!" shouts Kika. "He's not that kind of a dog!"

The creature stops. His nose twitches.

"I'm not?" asks Sniff. "I mean, no, I'm not. I like gophers! A lot!"

Kika glares.

"And … gophery-looking things too! I would never eat a gopher. Too gamey."

The little fellow shrieks.

"I mean," says Sniff backtracking, " I've just … heard things … you know, at the shelter and such … Really – I 'm nice. I'll never smell your butt again. I'm not a typical … uh … Uptop dog. I'm an … Underdog!"

"Underdog?" asks the creature suspiciously.

Kika rolls her eyes.

"Definitely," continues Sniff. "I like ballet. I'm meek and mild – and vegan!"

"Vegan." says the being inching closer. "Really?"

"Yes. Very much so."

"Hmmm. Well … all right." Squinting, he approaches Sniff to get a better look. "Is Dog your first name or your last name?"

"Neither. My name is Alan."

"Alan." Taking off his glasses and cleaning them with the hem of his sweatshirt, he says to Kika, "How about you, sir?"

Aww, man.

"Kika," she states. "I'm a girl."

"Okay." He fits his specs back over his dinky ears.

"And," begins Sniff, "you are …"

"Abahoe-Gopheem-Bozwell – buuuuutttt …" The creature flips up his hood and tugs down on his baggy jeans. He sticks out his booty, shimmies his shoulders and gyrates in a most lively fashion.

"You can call me Boogie Boy Boz,

The Bozterman,

or just because

my name's not Kevin, Stu, or Stan.

My moves are killa,

but my rap is chilla.

The Wizard of Boz! Bozooka! I'm
Vanilla Bozilla!
Or … um … *Todd* is fine."

"Not Boz?" asks Sniff.

"That's my stage name."

Curiouser and curiouser.

"So, hey," Todd chirps, "are you two hungry?"

"Yes!" barks Sniff.

"Uh … sure," answers Kika.

"Excellent. I'll take you to the Market. But first, we gotta clean you guys up. You stink. Let's get to the Grotto before it's jammed."

Sniff pokes Kika behind the knees with his cold wet nose. She meets his panicky eyes. He mouths, "Bath?" Sniff hates water in general and baths in specific.

"Uhh, Todd?" ventures Sniff. "I think I'm good."

"Good and grody," he snorts.

Sniff looks pleadingly at Kika. Uncertain, she

gives a little shrug. Resigned to his fate, the dog sighs.

The three amble along, rubble crunching under their feet as they zigzag through a maze of tunnels.

"Look at this, Sniff!" cries Kika. "An underground stream!"

"Yes, Kika," he replies, forgetting about The Bath for a moment. "As a matter of fact, that water dissolving this rock creates these caverns and tunnels."

"Up around North Darkoda," adds Todd, "the creek turns into a river."

"Gee," muses Kika. Glittery ripples bubble in her glow-globe's beam. "Todd?" she asks. "What's that I'm hearing?"

"What?" says Todd.

"That. Wait. It stopped. I guess it's just the stream splashing over the stones. No ... there it is again. It sounds like whispering and giggling.

"Creek geeks," says Todd. "And stream demons – our solution to pollution. They keep the stream clean by blasting the nasties. Freaky little dudes, but practically harmless."

"Practically," mutters the mutt as he tests the water with his paw. Finding the depth doable, he springs to the opposite bank like a stone skipping over a pond. Kika tiptoes quickly across with Todd following.

Safely on dry land, Sniff obsesses about his impending wet ordeal. Delaying it as long as possible, he dawdles. He sits and scratches. He smells rocks. He stops, cocks his head, and pretends to be listening to something important. Lagging farther and farther behind, he finally flops onto the dirt and doesn't move. Todd and Kika double back.

"You okay, boy?" she asks.

"Just taking time to enjoy the scenery," he says sprawling out.

Todd and Kika share a moment.

"So, Todd," says the dog brightly. "Tell us about yourself. What's your story? I hope it's a long one."

CHAPTER 5

"Ahh, the captivating saga of the Aba-hoe Nation," says Todd. "But before I begin, I must procure proper accompaniment."

He shrugs off his tiny knapsack and digs through it. Reaching deep, he whisper-sings a little Bob Dylan. *"Hey Mr. Tambourine man …* Tambourine. Um-hum. Definitely."

He yanks out a xylophone. "Uh, no."

He examines a harmonica. "Never could get the hang of this. Dental interferenth."

He shows Kika a pair of colorful castanets.

"Wanna join me?"

"I … don't know how," she replies relieved.

Todd proceeds to extract an astounding array of items from his marvelous pack. Sniff and Kika look on dumbfounded as a gong appears followed by three pairs of rhythm sticks, a triangle, two recorders, a ukulele, three sleigh bells, a pick-axe, and miscellaneous office supplies.

"Finger cymbals?" Todd ponders. "That would be a definite maybe. Hey, Alan, can you play anything?"

"I can play dead."

"Hmm. Good to know."

Todd crams everything back into his bag except for the tambourine, a silver referee whistle, and a pair of crude little drums tethered together.

"Gotta bop the bongos, man, to keep the beat sweet," he jives. With a flourish of drumfire and whistle tweet, Todd begins his tale,

> "Way back then, when Mama Earth was just a big blue blob,
> there lived this crazy cat named Steve – like, man, that cat was God.

Andrew and Amanda were Steve's twin little squirts.
They all lived semi-happily together in a yurt."

"What's a *yurt*?" breaks in Kika.

"A Mongolian tent," answers Sniff, "often constructed of animal ski – he checks himself hastily – Never mind."

"Where's their mother?" asks Kika.

"Divorced," says Todd sadly. "The family lived Uptop. She lived Downbottom."

"Kika," mouths Sniff peeking up mischievously. "He said *bottom*."

"Behave yourself," she giggles under her breath.

Wondering what was so stinkin' funny, Todd/Boz, continues,

"These little ankle-biters were, like totally annoying.
What toy one had, the other wanted, finally destroying

all their fluffy puffy animals. They
ripped them all in two.
Their pad was strewn with cotton guts. Ya
dig? Like really strewn.
Things began to escalate when these brats
hit their tweens.
Their bickering turned deadly, man – a really
messed-up scene.
No little plastic plushies did they mangle
like before.
They caught real living creatures for
their whacko tug-o-war."

"Eww," blurts Kika.
"Little psychopaths, those two."
"Eww. Eww."
"Ewe is right and bunny, too, and gopher,
rat, and badger bods trashed up the forest floor!"
Sniff licks his arm and then settles into
grooming his pads. Noticing the dog's waning interest, the little poet cranks it up. He rattles the
tambourine rebelliously and goes on,

"'Okay, that's it!' Big Steve went ape.
'You creeps I'm gonna separate!'
He never liked them all that much,
especially with each other.
'Andrew, you're Uptop with me. Amanda,
with your mother.'
'Oh, Dad,' the ghastly godlets whined.
'One up and one below?'
'You bet. Now clean your woods and take
these corpses when you go.'"

Sniff nods off.

Glancing over, Boz presses on valiantly, "The
kids felt really bad. They were totally sorry for
their uncool behavior and also, they missed bug-
ging each other.

Banished to their rooms, for days and days,
they cried and cried.
Then Compassion's loving flash hit hard and
lit them up inside.
When their tears of true remorse dripped on
the tiny creature parts,

it magically grew back those legs and eyes and tails and heads and guts and hearts."

Sniff is now dream-running.

"Anyway," says the Abahoe, trying to ignore the twitching dog body, "this made the twins feel really good, and they actually turned into extremely groovy gods. Andrew became head honcho Uptop and Amanda ruled the Abahoes Downbottom."

"What happened to Steve?" asks Kika.

"Well, since he now had tons of time on his hands, he spent most of it wooing fairy queens and forest nymphs."

"Oh," says Kika hoping that last word never shows up on a spelling test.

For his grand finale, Boz pops the whistle back into his mouth and blows 'til it squeals. He bangs his fist on the bongos in one last frenzy of inspiration. With his other hand, he shakes the tambourine to within a jingle of its life. He tosses it into the air and lets it crash to the ground, accidentally on purpose near the dozing dog.

Sniff jerks. Kika applauds. Sniff stretches. Todd staggers to his feet and takes a humble bow.

"Todd," yawns Sniff, "how long until we get to the Grotto?"

Kika narrows her eyes and glares. *Not cool, Sniff.* He catches her look.

In disappointed silence, the Abahoe's bushy little head droops. He shoves the instruments back into his pack and mumbles, "We're almost there." Sadly slinging his knapsack over his shoulder, he scuffs down the path.

"Todd, wait," calls Sniff. "Thanks for sharing your story, man. It was very entertaining and energetic. I enjoyed it."

"You did? Really?"

"Really."

Todd's face lights up like a sunrise. With a skip in his sneaks, he whoops, "Onward to the Grotto!"

Sniff gulps.

CHAPTER 6

"Pee-yew!" coughs Kika crinkling her nose. "Something smells like rotten eggs."

"Sulfur," informs Sniff. "An element often found in thermal springs."

They follow Todd through a narrow passageway. A muggy mist swirls around them as they enter the Grotto. The cavern is lined with *nichos* carved into its walls. Each holds a lump of glowing rock that illuminates the most wondrous sight – an underground pool. Shimmering turquoise water sparkles like aquamarines. Steam rises from its surface. A waterfall sends up a dazzling spray.

"Looks pretty empty now," says Todd, "but it'll be nuts later with everyone sprucing up for the festival. You guys ready?"

Fearing the inevitable, Sniff presses his trembling shoulders against Kika's calves. She removes his headlamp and her own, slips out of her flip-flops, and slowly unfastens the backpack. Even more slowly, she peels off her sweatshirt. Stepping carefully to the water's edge, she dips her toes. It feels divine. "What are you waiting for?" asks Todd.

"Umm …" begins Kika shyly.

"Oh, I get it. You can keep your clothes on. So, how 'bout you, Alan?"

"I don't much care for water. Childhood trauma. Unfortunate episode involving a garden hose."

"Sorry, bro. So, I'm gonna boogie on over to that lifeguard station and perfect my kazooing skills. Later, gator." He grooves away through the drizzle.

"Come on, Sniff," says Kika. "Don't be a puppy. The water's not that deep. Stand next to me and I'll pour a little over you."

"Not on my face!"

"Okay, not on your face."

"Fine." He marches stiffly in.

"See? That's not so bad."

"Just do it," he grumbles.

Kika fills her bottle and lets it gently spill over Sniff's back.

"Nice, right?"

"No."

They carefully wade in up to the dog's chest.

"Hang out here for a little while," she says. "You'll get used to it. I'm going to take a quick swim." Kika dives under, and then bobs to the surface. The silky water feels like a warm hug. Floating along, she closes her eyes and thinks, *Mmmm, I wish I could stay here forever!* Over the gurgling of the spring, she hears the most glorious sound. Singing – like a choir of angels. She lifts her head. It stops. Underwater, it continues, sweet and bewitching.

Kika paddles toward the falls. Rolling over, she plunges and surfaces behind a watery sheet of rippling glass. She glides forward to a sheltered cove where she discovers three of the most stunning young women – teenagers! They sit waist-deep in the bubbling pool humming and untangling each other's long hair with ornate ivory-colored combs. One raises her head. Her kelp-green eyes meet Kika's hazel ones, and she purrs, "Kika, right?"

"Um … Yes. How did you …"

"We know," she replies, all mysterious.

"What kind of name is Kika?" chirps another.

"It's my …"

"Anyway, I'm Juli. This is Tori and that's Lani."

Juli's straight licorice-dark hair tumbles to her bellybutton. Tori's cinnamon curls glisten in the grotto's wavering light, while Lani's shine like ribbons of caramel. The girls' kohl-smudged eyes contrast strikingly with their pale, luminous skin. Two of them dress in clothes left behind by Aba-hoe bathers. Tori's halter-top is made from a torn

T-shirt. Lani has on a scrap of beach towel. Juli wears her hair.

"Kika," says Lani. "I think your name is sweet. It sounds like candy. Good enough to eat."

"Well," says Tori, not to be outdone. "I love your swimsuit, Kika. So edgy."

"Oh ... um ... it's not really a ...Thank you," says Kika. "I swam over here because I heard your singing under the water. Your voices sound ..."

"Aren't we wicked fantastic?" yips Lani.

"Dork," smirks Tori splashing her in the face.

"Dweeb," Lani retorts with a water chop drenching Tori and also Kika.

"Ladies, ladies," chides Juli. "What were you saying, Kika? I wasn't listening."

Kika's face crumples.

"Oh Kika," Juli laughs. "I was only teasing."

The others titter.

Kika thinks it's awesome that these glamorous teens are actually talking to her, but they *are* a little intimidating, but maybe that's how cool girls act and she's being a little baby. She really wants them to like her. "Your voices sound wonderful," she gushes.

"Thank you," says Juli. "You're a honey."

"Honey," repeats Tori.

"Yummy," says Lani.

Juli glares at her.

"Uhh," says Kika, unclear about what just happened. "Are you guys from Uptop too?"

"Kind of," says Tori, "but we live here now."

"This is your residence?" asks Kika in her most grown-up way.

"Mm-hmm," murmurs Juli.

"Wow." That's all Kika could think of to say.

Picking out strands of waterweed and pond gunk, the teens continue to fix each other's hair. They whisper among themselves, occasionally looking up at Kika and smiling in an unsettling way. Not sure of what to do, Kika grins back and tries to engage them in conversation that doesn't sound stupid. "Your hair is amazing," she says. "I wish mine was long and …"

"Oh, Kika," laughs Juli. "Your hair is fresh and sassy."

"Fresh," says Tori licking her lips.

"And saucy," says Lani.

The others flash her a look.

"Kika!" barks Sniff from outside the falls.

"What is *that*?" asks Juli, all peeved.

"My dog," replies Kika, embarrassed. "He's fine. Don't pay any attention to him."

"Okay, we won't."

They seem to be ignoring Kika too. Disappointed in herself for not being cool enough, Kika sighs and turns away.

"Wait!" cries Juli. "I'm sorry. We're being rude. Hey, I know. Do you want to hear a secret?"

"We've never told this to anyone," says Tori flipping her hair around.

"Sure," says Kika, relieved to be included again. She wades back to join them.

"So," begins Juli, "like you, Kika, we used to live Uptop." She goes on to say how the three of them had been besties since elementary. They spent summer vacations together swimming in a beautiful lake, pretending they were dolphins and mermaids and Navy SEALs. By the light of the full moon, they imagined they were splashing through silver. Their dream was to float and play and sing in that lake forever. "And," continues Juli, "never take another pop quiz again, or listen to our annoying parents, or babysit our gross little brothers."

Juli's soothing voice, the warm water, and the gentle whooshing of the falls is making Kika drowsy. She pinches the inside of her elbow to stay awake as the story continues:

On an August night of their fifteenth year, a meteor shower streaked through the sky. The teens wished on every one for their secret desire to become a reality. "The next morning," finishes Juli, "our dream had come true, but we never walked the land Uptop again."

"Umm," begins Kika, wondering if she missed something. She suspects she might have been sleeping with her eyes open. "I don't really get it?"

The teens slowly lift their knees. Through the bubbles, they appear to be wearing shiny black leggings. Out of the water, Kika sees that they aren't leggings at all. They're scales. The lovely singers are – eels?

"Oh!" gasps Kika, springing back. "I'm – sorry?"

"Don't be," says Juli. "It's awesome being pond goddesses. Right, you guys?"

"Totally," says Tori.

"Hey, Kika," shouts Lani. "You wanna join us? Trade our fins for your feet? They're big enough."

"Shut up Lani," snickers Tori.

"What Lani means," begins Juli, her hungry gaze never leaving Kika's face, "is that we heard your wish of wanting to float in this glorious spring forever. You're so adorbs and nice, we were just wondering if you'd like to swap your boring little eleven-year-old life for ours?
To have long, incredible hair, and learn super-model make-up tricks, and always be a popular tween."

"What do you say, Keek?" tweets Lani.

"Well," Kika starts uncomfortably. "I'll think about it."

"Listen to our new song, then! We're auditioning for a major animation studio."

"But," says Kika, "didn't they make that movie already? The one about the mer …"

"This is the mini-series."

"Oh."

"High C's, girlfriends," orders Juli. "One, two. One, two, three, four …"

"If you wish upon a star,
just remember who you are.
You could make a nifty wish,
then turn out to be a fish!
Just be grateful. That's our motto,
or be living in a grotto.
If you want a dream come true,
This is what you have to do –
Make a wish and make it sweet.
Then, get up and move your feet!
So remember what we've said.
Wish upon yourself, instead.
Wish upon yourself instead."

"So, Keek," says Lani in a disturbing little girl voice, "what did you think of our song? Weren't we precious?"

"Lani, please stop talking," snarks Tori.

"KIKA!" barks Sniff impatiently.

"Umm," says Kika, "I think I better check on him."

"Oh, no, Kika, don't leave. Not yet, please?" purrs Juli slithering closer. "I want to share this super wonderful idea with you."

"Well ... okay, I guess," says Kika uneasily, "but I only have a minute."

"Of course. We understand," says Juli, glancing at the others. "You're so talented, Kika, and you have such great taste ..."

Lani giggles.

"... in *clothes*. Why don't you stay for just a tiny little bite – bit – and make our costumes?"

"Yay, Kika! Yay!" cries Lani, her open mouth revealing two dainty pointy teeth.

"Freak," sneers Tori.

"Don't you want to be one of the cool girls?" asks Lani, distressingly close. "Designer to the Stars?"

When Tori slides in, their nearness turns scary.

"It will be delicious," coos Juli.

"Delicious," echoes Tori, a dab of spit moistening her pretty lips.

"I really can't …" starts Kika.

"Sure you can …"

"KIKAAAAAAA!" howls Sniff.

"I gotta go," snaps Kika.

"Wait!" cries Juli grabbing at her.

Using her big flipper feet, Kika pushes hard off the bottom and kicks away.

"See Tori!" hisses Lani. "There she goes. You are such a loser."

"Me? You're the one who lost her!"

"Both of you are total idiots!" screams Juli, going after them.

They wriggle away in a bickering boil.

Like a torpedo, Kika blasts through the falls and breaststrokes back to Sniff who's exactly where she left him. "Where did you go?" he whines. "I've been standing in this water forever. My pads are all pruney. Are we done here?"

"Yes," says Kika breathlessly. "We are *done*."

"Finally."

"You were very brave, Alan," she says distractedly.

"Whatever," he says, splashing back to the beach.

Kika briskly scrubs her arms and legs and dunks her head again. She hears nothing but the burbling spring. Quickly sloshing up onto the sand, she finds her bottle, tucks it into the backpack, and slips on her thongs.

Todd and his kazoo wait onshore. Sniff blasts him with a shake. "Easy, Al. I already took one shower today! Ha ha ha!"

"Todd?" starts Kika urgently. "When I was underwater, I heard something."

"What?"

"Singing."

"Dude! You heard The Sirenas of the Springs? I thought they disappeared like a hundred years ago."

"A hundred years?" she gasps.

"At least."

"But, I just saw them."

"Zikes!" Todd blats his kazoo for emphasis.

"They sang me a song."

"Uh-oh. Did they try to get you to do something?"

"Sort of …"

"What?" he asks intensely. His glasses slip down his nose, but he doesn't bother to push them back up.

"They wanted me to stay with them," says Kika.

"Until the end of time, right?"

"I don't know. I didn't stick around long enough to hear the details."

"Right move, Ki. Those babes are slick."

"And mean," adds Kika.

"And they suck," says Todd.

"What sucks?" chirps Sniff who's always interested in anything to do with eating or drinking.

"Kika just met up with some bad *muchachas*," says Todd adjusting his specs. "Ki, listen. How do you think those three have stayed young for so long?"

She shrugs. "I don't know."

"Okay, it's pretty creepy," says Todd in a

chilling voice. "But, after they lure in their victims with their singing, Sirenas suck the life out of them and then carve their bones into combs for their hair."

"Oh, no," gasps Kika.

"In other words," says Sniff, "they drink the vital fluid of their prey. Like leeches."

"Or bats," says Todd, "who live in ..."

"Caves," says Kika shuddering.

The three stare in wide-eyed silence.

"Oh!" cries Kika coming to, "Oh, no. No! That could have been me! If I had waited just ..."

"But you didn't Kika," interrupts Todd, "You didn't *wait*."

"I didn't ... wait," stammers Kika, trying to make sense of things.

"Ki," continues Todd, "you escaped those nasty suckers – whatever they are. You didn't fall for their slimy games."

"You were very brave," nuzzles Sniff.

"But I didn't feel brave! I felt scared. I just swam away."

"Sometimes," says Sniff, "the bravest thing

you can do is …"

"Get the heck out!" shouts Todd. "And that's what we're gonna do right now. You guys ready?"

"Definitely," yips Sniff.

Kika nods numbly. With shaky hands, she dries off with her sweatshirt, stuffs everything into her pack, and zips it up. Still uncertain about how courageous she really was, Kika knows one thing for sure: she's a lot more grateful for her boring little eleven-year-old life.

CHAPTER 7

"You two have had a majorly whacked-out morning," says Todd, "but at least you're clean – and, now you must be starving."

"I am," barks Sniff. "Didn't have breakfast."

Food is the last thing on Kika's mind, but to be a good sport, she agrees.

"To the Market, then!" cries Todd, a little over-enthusiastically. "I forgot to pick up veggies on my way home from work."

"So, Todd," inquires Sniff, "aside from pursuing your theatrical career, what is your occupation?"

Todd unzips his hoodie and points to the words ORE ELSE! printed on his tee. "I mine. You dig?"

"I do," replies the dog, "although I'm afraid it's more of an obsession with me."

Todd mines illuminum. This precious mineral is used to make glow-globes, the gleaming balls popping out of Abahoe foreheads. From living so long underground, Abahoe eyes, according to Todd, are "exthremely thenthitive" (extremely sensitive). Illuminum gives off the perfect amount of light. An Abahoe mother plugs a lump of it into her baby's tiny skull while it's still soft, thus creating the *glow-hole*.

"Yuck," comments Kika.

"Then," says Todd, "when our kids get bigger, we swap 'em out – the glow-globes, not the kids. Ha ha ha!"

Kika has nothing to add.

The three mosey along.

"Uh … Todd?" barks Sniff out of nowhere, "You don't really look all that much like a gopher. I mean, you kind of smell like one? But … sorry, bro."

"No worries," says Todd amiably. He explains that his ancestry is uncommonly quirky. The Abahoe race blends various burrowing animals with certain charismatic cavern trolls, and also ETs. He shrugs his little shoulders. "Guess I'm just a mutt. No offense, Al."

"None taken," says Sniff. "I, myself, am the product of a mixed marriage."

"Actually," adds Kika, "so am I."

"I never knew my father," muses Sniff.

"Mine's not around that much," sighs Kika.

Awkward.

"Well, then, there you have it," concludes Todd, thinking it wise to change the subject. "Ever been to the Farmers Market?"

"I went to one Uptop once," replies Kika.

"Well, I think you'll find this one somewhat more great."

Todd leads them into a decent-sized cavern whirling with activity. Abahoes of every kind meander about – rabbit creatures with longish ears and hints of tails poking from beneath their jackets, lanky weasel people doing business with

stocky mole creatures, badger, rat, and snake beings bustling through the aisles. All have glowglobes, and all are covered in a fine, whitish hair.

Produce stalls encircle the outer edge of the Market. They're lit by illuminum chunks strung together like Christmas lights. A jumble of voices cry out, "Roots and shoots! Roots and"…"Get yer supa dupa pupas!"…"We got the beet! We got the"… "Parsnips, sage, rosemary, and"… "Larvaaaaa! Fat juicy"…"Red red red radishes!"…"Greta's Grub 'n Pub! Go see Greta. Ya never ate betta!"

Kika glances down to see Sniff panting, "Rabbits and badgers and moles, oh my. Rabbits and badgers and …" Kika nudges him with her shin and whispers, "Sniff. You're drooling."

He sucks in his cheeks. "Sorry. Sorry. So sorry."

"So," pipes Todd, "do you two enjoy carrots?"

"Yummy," answers Sniff unenthusiastically.

"Excellent! Then, we'll start right here." They approach a little vegetable stand dug into the side of the cavern. "Hey Jen!" says Todd to the older weasel person within. "What's buzzin' cuzzin?"

"Oh, you," she smiles, wiping her hands on her apron.

"Slip me three of your finest sweet carrots, my sweet."

Jen stretches out her long torso, and reaches into the ceiling. "What size?" she asks.

"Small is fine for me," answers Todd.

"Me too," says Kika.

"I'll share," says Sniff.

Jennifer yanks down two plump golden beauties that had been growing out of the stall's roof.

Wow, thinks Kika, *I wonder if we're underneath Mr. Romero's garden.*

Brushing off the dirt, Jen hands the carrots to Kika and Todd. She peers at Sniff. "This is Alan," says Todd. "He's a vegan and fellow miner."

"Rock hound," murmurs Sniff.

"What is he?" Jen asks.

"I'm mostly Pit," interjects Sniff. "I mean, as in hole. I excavate."

"I see," she says, suspiciously.

"So, Jen," jumps in Todd hastily, "how are the boys?"

"Oh, you know – little weasels. All of 'em."

"Glad to hear it. Glad to hear it." Todd quickly pays in crystal chips and hustles the others along.

CHAPTER 8

"Todd! Wait!" cries Kika through the hubbub. "What's over there?"

She points to a platform at the center of things where a fashion show is underway.

"Mr. Wiggley's introducing his new fall line," says Todd.

"Ooooh!" squeals Kika, "Can we go see? I love clothes."

As they wind their way through the shoppers, Todd continues, "Everyone calls him the Web Master."

"Wait. What?" says Kika.

"Brilliant web designer."

"I'm confused." (for about the gazillionth time today).

"Worms," says Todd searching for a place to sit. "Webworms. Abahoe clothing is woven from their webs. It's way stronger than silk, and shinier. Wiggley's weavers are the best."

The three find seats near the back. Graceful serpent-like creatures vogue down the runway in the most fabulous outfits. Everything gleams white – the models' hair, their complexions, the fuzz on their skin, their gowns and tunics and tennis wear. A dapper little rat person stands at the podium enthusiastically emceeing the show.

"Ancient Greece," begins the designer, "is trending this season. It inspires the final creation in my fall collection. A simple toga? Of course, but so much more! Liz, luv, will you please demonstrate? Tie it around your waist – *voila*!! You've got a cover-up for a day at the Springs. Add a string of illuminum pearls and you're ready for the Grammys. A snazzy belt takes it from day to night. Around your neck, it's an oversized scarf. This must-have piece is a shawl, a sarong, a poncho, yoga pants, a drop cloth! Oh, the possibilities! I call it *Le Sheet Chic*. It lets you be the designer. Yes, oh yes, you too can be a wrap artist! Thank you, Liz. And thank you, ladies and gentlemen for your kind attention. The entire House of Wiggley autumn line may be viewed at stall 17."

"Wow!" says Kika. "How neat! I can't wait to show Mami how to tie those pants."

"Dogs don't do clothes," mentions Sniff.

The three weave back into the market. "Are there always so many Abahoes here?" asks Kika.

"Unh-uh," answers Todd. "Everyone's picking up last-minute stuff for Prismacus."

"Prismacus," says Sniff, pondering the word's origin.

"Our most holy happening," says Todd seriously. "Allow me to demonstrate." His little bag slides to the ground with a disturbing clunk. Turning his toes outward into ballet second position, he warms up with a few deep *plies*.

Kika and Sniff look on nervously.

"The festivities begin at dusk!" Todd, now Boz, proclaims, creeping around in his portrayal of Dusk.

He drops to a crouch. "Night falls." (not that you'd notice because it's underground).

Kika catches Sniff's eye and gestures, "What's he doing?"

Sniff mouths back, "Interpretive dance."

Boz pogos into the air, lands on one foot, and declares, "We celebrate through the night …"

The shoppers give him room.

"… with Thircuth Prithmacuth!"

The exuberant Abahoe leaps and pirouettes and pantomimes a variety of circus acts, his face a montage of ever-changing expressions. He stops abruptly. His gangly arms rise like butterfly wings to form a graceful arc overhead. "And then," he pronounces mysteriously, "The Incending!" Boz's upturned face frozen in wonderment, and his body rigid, he stands still for a really long time. The audience loses interest. Kika checks out a hangnail. Sniff considers scooting his butt along the ground, but thinks better of it. Boz snaps out of his dance trance and shouts, "Snacks!!!"

The girl and dog jolt.

"So Ki," continues Todd cheerily, "ever eat grubs?"

"Um, no. I mean, at a campout I ate grub but …"

"Well, you've never had 'em like you'll have 'em at my sister-in-law's."

They approach a beachy little purple, pink, and orange striped shack. Flags of many nations flitter from the rafters. Over the door hangs a spray-painted banner that reads, GRETA'S GRUB 'N PUB, and it features a frosty mug with a handle shaped like a laughing bloated worm.

The three take seats at the counter.

Greta appears in a swish of posies and polka dots. A froth of curls escapes from her elaborately-twisted headscarf.

"Li'l Bro!" she beams, a big grin pooching out her peachy cheeks.

"Hey Big Sis!" Todd air-kisses her. "Say hello to my new budds, Kika and Alan. They're visiting from Uptop."

"Pleased to meetcha." She greets them with a slightly oily hand/paw shake. "What'll y'all have today?"

"So, Al," says Todd, "you're not a total vegan, are ya?"

"No, no," says Sniff. "Not at all. I'm a lacto-larvo."

"Okie dokie then." Turning back to his sister, Todd orders, "Three dozen of your best, see vous please. Light on the cumin."

"Coming right up!" she cries.

"I hope not!" guffaws Todd.

"Oh, Toddy," giggles Greta, "you should be a stand-up comedian."

"I'm workin' on it, Gret," he winks. "I'm workin' on it."

Clucking and chuckling, the colorful little chef heads over to the fryer.

"So, Todd," says Kika, "Prismacus starts today?"

"Yep. Circus tonight and, tomorrow, the Incending at the exact moment of the autumnal equinox."

"I forget," says Kika. "What's that again?"

"An equinox," begins Sniff, distracted by Greta's grub prep, "is one of only two times in the year when day and night are equal in length – around September 22."

"Ki," says Todd." If you wanna do Prismacus like a real Abahoe, you have to bring something to barter."

"Barter," interjects Sniff. "To trade – goods and/or services."

"Oh," says Kika, a little concerned about this new development. "So, Todd, what are you bartering?"

"Ballads from my new rock opera about the inventor of TNT. Gonna be dynamite! Ha ha ha! Hope I don't bomb!"

Greta sets down the steaming servings. "Ahh. I love di little grubs!" cries Todd peering over his glasses, which he swaps out for a pair of shades. He fluffs his dreads and vaults off the seat.

Curious about what's coming next, Kika smiles. Sniff struggles to stay on his stool.

Hips swaying, Boz, starts,

"I love di little grubs, mon.
Eat 'em wid mi budds, mon.
At di Greta's pub, mon.
Dub-a-Rub-a-Dub, mon."

He hops back up and chirps, "To be continued. Don't want lunch to get cold. Kika, I think you'll be impressed with the way Greta prepares these grubs – soft inside, crispy outside."

Kika peeks down in horror. Lunch looks like a wad of french-fried rubber bands. A stink resembling belly button jam swirls up to assault her nostrils. Stomach somersaulting, she wonders how she'll survive this sickening ordeal. Not fazed, Sniff inhales his.

"Aren't they a gas?" says Todd.

"Yes they are," burps Sniff. "Taste like chick – I mean, Tofurky."

"Todd," says Kika, "do you maybe have ketchup?"

"Negativo. How 'bout Stevia?"

"That's okay."

Pretending to eat, Kika pushes the ghastly things around in her bowl. She glances at Sniff who glares at her. "Be polite and try it," he mouths, a silvery-green glop oozing off his black, bottom lip.

She spears a loathsome larva. "Aaaack!" she screams. "It wiggled!"

"Medium rare," Todd enthuses through a gooey gob.

Sniff gives Kika a warning poke. "Okay. Okay," she whispers. Discretely holding her nose,

 she parts her lips and shoves in a forkful really fast. She chews. *Pop, pop, pop.* Kika doesn't even want to *know* what's going on inside her mouth right now. She swallows hard. A mo-

ment later, she feels tickling at the back of her throat. She coughs into her hand and gapes as a tough little grub inches off her palm and falls onto the floor.

"So?" asks Todd.

"Yummy," chokes Kika trying not to be a pain.

"Wash it down with this," he says helpfully. Todd hands her a mug of something that looks like mulch floating in pickle juice, and smells like armpits.

Kika sips. It is *so* bad. "What's …" she gags through watering eyes.

"Radical Roots Beer," he says proudly. "Greta's most popular micro-brew."

"Oh," says Kika picking a sliver of turnip pulp off her tongue. "It tastes different than …"

"Kika," interrupts Sniff jovially, "if you're full, I'll finish your lunch for you."

"Thank you!" she cries with relief.

Bam! Her bowlful is history.

Todd waves to Greta. "Thanks Sis! You've outdone yourself!"

She blows him a kiss. Todd wipes his mouth on his sleeve. "So, kids, I gotta make like a drum and beat it. Ha ha ha. I'm on the decorating committee."

"But," barks Sniff. "Where are we going?"

"Amanda's Cavern, dude."

"How do we get there?" asks Kika anxiously.

"Just follow your feet, Ki. The gravel ghosts know the way, but, hey, man, be careful. They've usually got an agenda."

CHAPTER 9

"*Follow my feet,*" says Kika, her forehead puckering in worry. "Sniff, what did Todd mean by that?"

"Search me. I follow my nose."

"And gravel ghosts!" she cries, her big eyes growing bigger. "What are those? What if they're dangerous? What if we get lost? What if we never …"

Kika's heart thumps madly. She shivers in an icy sweat. Her breath comes in shallow gasps and her stomach leaps up into her throat. The backpack feels like a boulder over her shoulders. A swell of dizziness washing over her, she stumbles.

"Kika?" says Sniff. "What's wrong? You're white as an Abahoe."

Kika shakes her head, unable to speak. Sniff guides her to a quiet alcove. Knees buckling, she melts to the earth. The dog gentles up next to her and sits. His little ears tuck back and concern darkens his watchful eyes.

A fat tear plops onto the dirt and forms a perfect crater. "Sniff?" Kika whimpers, "Am I sick?"

"No, no, Kika," he says relieved that she can talk again. "You're not sick. It's just that when some people get overwhelmed, this can happen."

It's easy for a person like Kika to get overwhelmed because she's an expert worrier. She stresses about things that happened that weren't her fault and things that might happen that probably won't. *I hope I'm not late. I hope I'm not weird. Why can't I understand long division? What will happen if I don't get a hundred percent on my spelling test?*

Sniff stands by. After a bit, he coaxes gently,

"Kika, do you think you might be able to take a few deep breaths?"

She inhales haltingly and then loses it again, her mind spinning with awful thoughts. Sniff pauses for her to chill and then pokes his nose up under her hand. "Kika," he says softly, "will you please pet my head?" She does.

"Did you know that you can't pet my head and be scared at the same time?"

"Unh-unh," says Kika calming down with every stroke.

Sniff licks the tears off her wet cheeks. A giggle escapes from her lips. "Your breath smells like grubs."

"Forgot to floss," he grins. "Feeling better?"

"A little," she hiccups, feeling better for about a second. "But, Sniff? Will you take us home?"

"First of all, no," he replies, "and second of all, stop being a weenie."

Kika snuffs miserably.

"Kika," continues the dog, "What do you do at home?"

She shrugs.

"Exactly. You bore yourself to death waiting around for something to happen, or you cry about wanting to be somewhere else. Well, this is the Somewhere Else!"

Sniffle. Kika thinks about everything she's dreaming to do when she's a teenager and everything she's not doing now because she's so busy waiting for then. To do nothing now because you're waiting to do something later suddenly seems silly and wasteful and also, wussy.

"It's called an Adventure, Kika," continues Sniff doggedly. "It's the opposite of waiting. And, it's not boring."

Adventure. Kika has always liked the sound of that word. Exotic locales, handsome heroes in really dirty clothes, evil hags, dangerous situations, wicked kings, lots of long hair and many strapless gowns. But she figured that adventures only happened to people like Dora and Alice and Milo and Harry. Could she, Kika, actually have an adventure of her own? The thought gives her goose bumps.

"Okay," she says finally. "I'll try it, even

though I'm a wimp."

"You are also wonderful." Sniff snuggles his muzzle into Kika's ear.

She hugs him 'til he squirms. Her heart has quieted and she feels, if not courageous, at least curious. She notices an annoying nudging around her ankles and wonders if it's those gravel ghosts. Before she can react, it stops.

"So," she tells Sniff gamely, "might as well check out this Prismacus thing."

Paw pump. "Yes!"

"But, Sniff," says Kika catching herself mid-whine, "we don't have any goods and/or services to barter."

"Excuse me?" he says. "Kika, what are you great at?"

"I don't know."

"Not an answer."

"I suppose I draw pretty well."

"You're fantastic!" he yips.

"I guess," she admits. "But, what about you?"

"Moi?" he sighs dramatically. "Oh, if I absolutely must, I'll recite Shakespeare."

Whaaaat?

"Or I could do …" His upper lip curls disdainfully. "Tricks … possibly both … hmm … a *command* performance … Kika, give me a command."

"Sit."

Sniff poses regally, and in an English accent, he intones, "From *Richard II* – 'Let us SIT upon the ground and tell sad stories.' Sounds like you, Kika. "

"Oh, wow, Sniff. Where'd you learn to do that?"

"YouTube. Another command, *por favor.*"

"Umm … Beg?" she says.

"Is that a question?"

"Beg!"

Sniff rears up on his haunches. *"A Midsummer Night's Dream* – 'What worse place can I BEG in your love than to be used as you use your dog.' Sounds like me."

"Shake!" she giggles. He lifts his paw elegantly. *"Sonnet 18* – 'Rough winds do SHAKE the darling buds of May.'"

Kika laughs. "All right, Sir Woolypads, let's go do this Adventure."

The gravel ghosts, tired of waiting for Kika and Sniff to *process*, have taken another assignment and leave the two travelers to find Amanda's Cavern on their own.

CHAPTER 10

Kika takes the lead as she and Sniff thread out of the market. Ahead, she spots a wide tunnel lit by illuminum lanterns. A murmur of festively-clad Abahoes passes by in stunning white costumes – men in tunics – men in tutus – women in long, silky dresses and capes.

"Don't you love what everyone's wearing?"

"I don't know," says Sniff. "I'm looking down."

"Oh. Well, I'm pretty sure we're going the right way."

Mingling, they note quizzical stares and veiled whispers aimed in their direction. "Maybe they think we're celebrities," says Kika.

"Or serial killers," offers Sniff.

Though Kika is one of the tallest girls in her class, being among creatures that only come up to her ribs feels strange. Slouching down so she won't frighten them, she figures being as invisible as possible is the best plan in this situation. At home, this is Kika's plan in most situations.

She notices Sniff smiling angelically, his wide mouth stretched into a ridiculous grin. Swallowing often to prevent slobber from betraying his *inner dog*, he gazes up at Kika and bats his amber eyes sweetly. "Don't I look pleasant and harmless?"

Kika giggle-snorts.

The two pass quietly among Abahoes pushing carts filled with wares to barter: rank-smelling soups, stews and other food items, T-shirts, souvenir buttons, and refrigerator magnets. Some carry signs, babies, and bedding. All greet each other warmly, "Peaceful Prismacus!" Compared to the noise-riot of the market, Amanda's Passage is pleasantly low-key.

Kika feels tugging at her shorts.

"Are you going to eat that?" comes a marshmallowy voice. Kika looks down to see the dearest little creature staring up at her. The yellow nametag on her jumpsuit reads, *Hello. My name is Pammi* (with a happy face dotting the *i*).

Kika had forgotten Jen's carrot hanging out of her back pocket. She replies, "Uh, no, you can have it."

"Thanks, Kika" says Pammi, stashing it in her fanny pack.

"How did you know my name?"

"You're a celebrity."

Kika gives Sniff a *told-you-so* smile. He shrugs.

Pammi takes Kika's finger into her cool, dry hand. "I'm here to look after you and your friend Sniff."

"Alan." jumps in Sniff eagerly. "Canine-Hybrid-Alan."

Sniff seems very interested in the little Abahoe, and not just because she looks like a rabbit.

"Aww," says Pammi, "You're so *handsome*."

Sniff struts forward with a prance in his paws and a twirl in his tail.

"Are you related to the other Uptop dogs, Alan? The ones who live in burrows? The guards?"

"Prairie dogs." says Kika. "I don't think that ..."

"Yes, Pammi," barks Sniff, trying to fit in, and also impress the darling bunny babe. "I believe I am the larger, more mutant variety."

"You are very large, Alan."

When Sniff puffs out his big hairy chest, Kika chuckles on the inside, amused by her pal's cute flirtation.

The three meander along the less-trafficked side of the corridor.

Rubbing Kika's thumb affectionately, the tiny thing asks, "So, Kika, do you have any questions? Need some help? May I be of assistance? How 'bout a guidebook – GPS – Wet Wipes?"

"Uh," starts Kika. "I'm not sure."

"Take all the time you need," says Pammi.

She skips alongside Kika and whistles a happy tune.

"Well," starts Kika, "This is my first Prismacus ..."

"Aww. Are you excited? Nervous?"

"Both, I guess."

"You know, Kika, excited and nervous are actually the same thing – only one feels good and the other feels icky. So, what will you be sharing?"

"I'm going to draw, and Alan will ..."

"Pammi," interrupts Sniff, nudging himself between the two, "would you like to hear a love sonnet right now?"

"How sweet. Maybe later, Alan, but thank you." She scratches between the ears of the very blissed-out dog.

"How about you, Pammi?" says Kika, kind of hating to break the mood. "Will you be bartering at Prismacus?"

"Well, I don't have a special talent to trade, but I *will* be aiding and comforting. We of the Hareem clan are *carers* – taught to be kind to all creatures – even ones you don't like."

Kika understands this concept, but wonders if it applies to blood-sucking eel-girls.

Taking any opportunity to gaze into Pammi's pale denim-blue eyes, Sniff asks dreamily, "What about the other clans?"

Pammi explains that at Prismacus, all are invited to share their *theatrical* skills, but normally, each is known for what they do best. For example, Badgeems protect, Gopheems mine, Serpenteems are the thinkers and mystics, and Rateems create. "Sometimes, though," she adds, "a Rateem will be born who is an excellent salesman, or a Weaseem may have a gift for the occult. You never know."

"It's like that Uptop too," says Kika.

"Except without tails," adds Sniff knowingly.

Kika stares at him and shakes her head. Pammi tosses hers back and laughs gaily. Her fuzzy beret slips off and tumbles to the ground. Sniff rushes to retrieve it. Clasped between his teeny front teeth, he delicately returns the little hat to Pammi.

"Aww, thank you Alan," she smiles.

"Not a problem, Pammi," he replies, all Mr. Cool.

"So Kika," says the sweet Hareem, "Is there anything else you want to know about our celebration? I want you to feel comfortable."

"Well," she starts. "What's the Circus like? Are there clowns? What's in the stew? I want to know everything."

"Why?"

"I'm scared of surprises."

"We are on an *Adventure*, Kika," reminds Sniff smiling through clenched jaws.

"Oh," says Pammi, "then I'm afraid you must accept the first truth about Adventure, Kika."

"What's that?" she asks warily.

"Surprise."

Darn.

"You'll be okay, pretty girl. So, anyway, gotta bounce. Bye-bye."

"Bye-bye, Pammi!" shouts Sniff, a little over-the-top. "Have a nice Prismacus! ... Doggone it," he mutters. "Guess she didn't hear me."

"Sniff has a girlfriend, Sniff has a girlfriend," sings Kika.

"I do not," he barks petulantly. "That Pammi is just a really great gal."

CHAPTER 11

"O M Gosh," gasps Kika.

Amanda's Cavern opens before them. Giant fingers of translucent rock jut from the walls and ceiling. Their facets glisten like diamonds. Kika runs her palm along the cool glassy surface. "Sniff!" she cries. "It's crystal! This whole place is made of crystal!"

"Clearly," states the dog.

The cave curves around an elevated platform with an enormous quartz tower rising out of its center. Illuminum footlights flood the playing

area. It glows like moonbeams. White-clad Abahoes mill around the stage's base. Occasionally,
an official-looking Badgeem saunters through.
Kika and Sniff creep to an out-of-the-way spot to
watch everyone celebrating grandly – bartering,
frolicking, eating.

"I'm starving," says Kika.

Tucking himself under an overhang, Sniff
digs himself a shallow rest-pit, stretches out, and
settles his chin on his crossed wrists.

"Snifferton," she repeats, "I'm really hungry."

"Woof," he yawns.

"Oh, don't go all *dog* on me. I need your help
to get some food … Pleeeze, Alan?"

Sniff gazes up placidly, a little half-moon
showing at the bottom of his dark eyes.

"Bow wow."

"Okay, fine. I get it. You want me to do something all by myself, right? Teach me a stupid les-
son? Fine."

Attacking the backpack, Kika rummages for
her sketchbook and pencil. Her mind fumes, *So,*

Sniff, you don't think I can do this. But, you are so wrong. And I'm gonna prove it. Just watch me, Dog. Listen and learn!

"Sketches for supper?" starts Kika.

"Seriously?" says Sniff.

"What now?"

"Uh … Louder, maybe? So someone can actually hear you? Like you're *hungry*?"

"All right, all right," she grumbles. "How's this – Sketches for supper! Sketches for supper!"

"Better," mutters the dog, returning his jaw to his paws.

"Sketches for supper!" she yells.

Kika quickly draws a crowd – or, rather, she *draws* the crowd. One after another, she sketches the eager Abahoes, many who are seeing themselves for the first time. One young Moleem asks her baby brother, "Do I really look like that?" "Yes you do," he answers, "only uglier."

From his place, Sniff observes the action. He's also on the lookout for Pammi.

The Abahoes trade generously – not only foodstuffs, but illuminum earrings, bracelets, rings, pins, two capes, and a tutu.

While Kika sketches a cute young Rateem named Chev, he sings her this old Irish sea shanty (try saying *that* three times fast):

"I stowed away when I was ten onto the
Molly B.
I threw away the life I had for one upon
the sea.
For one upon the sea, hey-ho,
For one upon the sea.
I scrubbed the spuds. I swabbed the deck.
I did as I was told.
I earned me keep in grog and in doubloons
of pirate gold.
I traveled all around the world from
Ecuador to France.
I learned to whittle poisoned darts and
how to hula dance.
And how to hula dance, hey-ho,
And how to hula dance.
I charmed the snakes in India and lassies
from the Isles.

I ate with chopsticks and I rode a camel up
the Nile.
Upon the Seven Seas I sailed,
beholdin' wondrous sights.
By day, I lived out all the dreams I dared to
dream at night.
I dared to dream at night, hey-ho,
I dared to dream at night.
A mighty storm took *Molly* down. Before she
sank, I cried,
Me life was merry, fine, and grand! I LIVED
until I died.
I LIVED until I died, hey-ho,
I LIVED until I died!"

"That was great!" cries Kika handing Chev
his drawing. "Thank you."

"Thank *you*, Kika, for my portrait," he
replies, kissing her hand. He asks for her number.

Kika's heart flits like fireflies. A rosy heat
starts at her toes and fizzes up through her body
to color her cheeks.

"Kika! Kika!" interrupts Greta flouncing onto

the scene. "Wanna trade a picture for a month of gruburgers?"

Sniff's ears perk up.

"Uh, sure, Greta," replies Kika, distracted. "I'll be right with you." Turning back to darling Chev, she sighs, "Sorry." He lifts his shoulders, makes a little disappointed face, and drifts away. Kika follows him with her eyes before dashing off a quick sketch for Greta.

Before Kika can feel sad about her almost romance, or go get a snack, a strangely-alluring being slides up next to her. Thin and willowy, it appears both male and female. His-her satiny skirt rustles beneath a safari jacket. Exotic, slanted eyes smolder with a violet flame. Through pillowy lips, a husky voice croons, "I am the Mysterious Serpenteem Mel. If you'd care to trade with me, your fortune I will tell."

"Okay," says Kika, enchanted by this fascinating presence.

The oracle takes Kika's hand, and with eyes closed, he-she chants,

"I see a teen dressed all in white
who's having such a super night.
Her friends are gathered 'round her chair.
I even see a boyfriend there.
This girl is smart. She knows her mind.
She's confident, and she is kind.

Mel pauses. "The vision blurs. Let me adjust the antenna." Illuminum bangles jangle as the medium lifts his-her arm. He-she rubs between Kika's eyebrows. "Ah yes, all becomes sharp. So anyway,

For this prediction to come true,
there's something that this girl must do.
She has a Light inside herself
that speaks to her and no one else.
And, if she listens to her Light,
she'll always know which way is right.
When she is scared and full of doubt,
she'll ask her Light to help her out.
She'll feel its answer in her heart
or in some other body part.

She'll ask her Light, 'Is this a *Yes*?'
then listens to inside her chest.
And if the *Yes* feels strong and clear,
she can go forward without fear.
But if the *Yes* feels more like *No*,
she's also found her way to go.

Kika, this girl is you."

Duh.

"Remember, if it's not *Yes*, it must be *No*. Trust your Light. You're good to go." The Mysterious Mel's dangly earrings quiver. He-she bobbles his-her bald tattooed head and shudders dramatically. "Can I have my drawing now?"

"Yes, of course," says Kika creating a lovely likeness and handing it to him-her.

Whew, thinks Kika. *That was a lot to take in. Not now, though. I'm way too psyched.*

"Sniff!" she shouts. "Look what I got! Such great stuff!" She spreads out the marvelous bounty and sits back in wonder. *I can't believe I earned all this myself. And I didn't have to be a teenager to do it!*

Famished, Kika grabs a slab of parsnip pie. "I think I'm done, though. My hand's cramping and I'm out of eraser. Plus, we have plenty." She takes a giant bite and, through a gooey mouthful, garbles, "Why don't you try, Sniff? It's totally fun."

From his spot, Sniff muses on the pointlessness of this endeavor … his belly is full, Kika is happy, Pammi won't be watching, and the Aba-hoes don't really like him. But just to please, because that's what dogs do, he plods out, sits up awkwardly on his hind legs, and half-heartedly intones, "Tricks for treats. Tricks for treats."

At the sight of a Dog – and a rather dull Dog at that – the crowd wanders off.

CHAPTER 12

"Sorry everybody left before your act, Sniff," says Kika, fastening one of the Abahoe capes around her shoulders.

"I'm relieved, actually," he replies. "Wasn't really feeling it. But I *am* feeling all those grubs I scarfed. I need grass."

"Uh-oh."

"I'll live," he burps.

Kika spins around. "Isn't this cape adorbs? Do I look like an Abahoe?"

"No."

"Let's tie this one around …"

"Noooo!" he whines.

"Oh, come on, you big poop."

"All right," he grouses.

Kika fits it loosely around his neck. "Aww, you're so *handsome*," she teases.

"I look like a …"

"Shhhh. Sniff; listen."

Silvery notes like delicate tapping on wine glasses, bring human, dog, and Abahoe to awed silence. An orchestra of Gopheems perched around the edge of the cavern play the clear quartz icicles with tiny mallets. Their music rises and falls – softer, then louder, still louder, until it crescendos in a rainbow of sound.

"Look over there," pokes Sniff. White-robed Moleems, balancing on stilts, materialize out of somewhere. They ceremoniously swing smoking pots of the most scrumptious scent. "What's in the buckets?"

Kika breathes in deeply. "I don't know, but it smells delicious. Cinnamon buns and *churros* and caramel corn."

Sniff sniffs. "I smell steak."

In unison, the crowd inhales. Kika feels a litle out-of-focus. Unaffected by the vapor, Sniff licks his elbow.

Through the fragrant mist, a pale form glides onstage. A twinkling tiara encircles her head like a halo. Her platinum gown glistens with illuminum stars. Vibrating with energy, her graceful Weaseem body shimmers and her jet-dark eyes dance. Abahoes nearby whisper, "Ooooh. There she is! Priestess Michelle! Isn't she awesome and sparkly?"

Michelle raises her lovely arms. The audience follows.

"Peaceful Prismacus!" she cries.

"Peaceful Prismacus!" they answer.

"May our joy bless this evening."

Kika sees that, instcad of applauding, the Abahoes have opened their mouths wide to let out a loud, whispery *haaaa* from way back in their throats. It sounds like the ocean. Neat, but kind of spooky.

The mistress of ceremonies continues, "I would like to extend a special welcome to our two visitors from Uptop – Kika and Sniff-Alan!!"

The crowd *haaspers* heartily.

"Kika," Michelle says, "and – well, no – just you, Kika dear, come up and introduce yourself."

Kika freaks. She turns to Sniff and whispers, "I can't."

He nudges her forward. "Yes you can. You're a celebrity!"

"There are so many people! I'm too nervous!"

"Nervous?" he asks.

"I mean – excited. Yes. Excited," she says, convincing herself. "I am very very excited …"

"Come on Kika," the priestess calls playfully. "We won't bite – much!"

The audience cracks up. "Ki-ka. Ki-ka. Ki-ka!" they chant.

Kika stands up straight and brushes a smear of dried pond scum off her T-shirt. Taking two giant belly breaths, she strides forward. A burly Badgeem helps her onto the platform, and Priestess Michelle leads her to center stage. Staring into a sea of glow-globes gives Kika an eerie but exhilarating feeling.

"So, young lady," begins the hostess, "tell us a little about yourself."

"Well … um. My name is Kika Jones? Kika Jones. Catalina Lucia Kika Jones. I'm eleven, I'm in middle school, and I live with my mother and my dog, Snifferton Alan Woolypads in New Mexico."

"New Mexico?" asks Michelle. "Is that in the United States?"

"Yes, Ms Priestess, it is," replies Kika.

"Who knew?" she titters.

The Abahoes hoot.

Michelle continues, "So, Kika do you have any hobbies?"

"I like to draw. And one day, I hope … I mean, I *plan* to be a fashion designer."

"Well, well," She winks. "Perhaps Mr. Wiggley can give you a few tips."

The Web Master stands on his seat and nods graciously as the throng cheers. He points to Kika and gives her a thumbs-up. Grinning, Kika returns the gesture.

"Oh, my," says Michelle. "So, Kika, thanks

for sharing. Let's hear it for Kika Jones!"

The crowd *haaspers* with gusto.

"Peaceful Prismacus!" cries Kika loving all the attention.

"Yes, yes," says the hostess moving along. "Peaceful Prismacus, Peaceful Prismacus. Thank you, Kika."

"Thank you, Michelle," says Kika waving to the crowd.

"Uh, Bruce, will you escort Miss Jones to her seat now?"

Kika skips back to Sniff, her cape billowing like a sail.

"You were great!" he yips.

"I didn't look like a dork?"

"No. You looked like you were having fun."

"I was."

Kika had been so into her experience onstage that she forgot to be scared.

"It really *was* exciting, Sniff."

I guess, realizes Kika, *that sometimes it's worse thinking about doing something than actually doing it.*

Amanda's priestess continues, "So dear Aba-hoes, and Othereems, without further ado, I present The Greatest Show Under Earth – Circus Prismacus!!!"

BADDA BONG!

Kika and Sniff jump. Out of the audience march brawny Badgeems in dazzling white uniforms pounding on instruments made from hollow roots, river stones, and other things. They station themselves around the skirt of the platform, clacking and scratching and banging out a lively repertoire.

The cavern throbs. Sniff holds back a howl.

A troupe of ghostly contortionists *cha-cha* onto the platform and twist their long bodies into letters that spell CIRCUS PRISMACUS.

The crowd *haaspers* in delight.

On gauzy hanging silks, graceful acroBa-teems perform a wondrous aerial ballet.

Jugglers in snowy tights race up and down the cavern walls sending a swarm of fiery spheres buzzing through the air. Tossing them at impossible angles and incredible speeds, they whiz into a blur.

"Sniff," whispers Kika, "it's like being inside an atom!"

"Yes, Kika, it is," he says distractedly. Sniff is having a difficult time with the circus. The commotion makes him tense, drumming hurts his ears, his tummy's upset, and he really hates the cape.

BLAAAAAT!

A dozen Hareem clowns in baggy white shorts saunter onto the stage. They trip over their giant feet, honk their red nose-balls, bonk each other over the head with kitchen utensils and fall down a lot.

The Abahoes roar.

What the heck are they laughing at? Kika doesn't get clowns.

As if hearing her thoughts, the Funny-Bunny Boyz reach behind their backs, pull skateboards out of their big pants and hop on. They careen down the aisles and back up onto the stage leapfrogging, somersaulting and tumbling in mid-air.

"Wahoo!" screams Kika. "Now that's what I'm talking about!"

One spectacle after another bursts through the arena. The intoxicating incense swirls magic into the air.

Bubbles like enormous iridescent balloons waft over the astonished audience. The Stupendous Serpentimi Sisters dip and swoosh huge circular wands, enclosing one another in glassy tubes of rippling soap. Then, like alabaster threads, they braid themselves into fancy patterns, mesmerizing with their slinky dance. Ever upward they slither around the spire, their glow-globes lighting its peak where enchanting Michelle appears behind a gigantic wiggling bubble. It pops. She giggles gleefully and cries, "Let's hear it for the hilarious Funny-Bunny Boyz, the rowdy jugglers, the flexible acroBateems, and everybody else!!!"

The crowd goes insane.

"Life," she sparkles, "is an excuse to celebrate!!!!"

Haaaaaaaaaaaaaaaaaaaaaaaaa!!!!

"Lovely, lovely, lovely. As High Priestess of Amanda, I now welcome all to this year's Incending."

Michelle closes her eyes in devotion.

"Anyhoo," she continues, "the equinox reminds us that though we are different as night and day, we are all equally different and thus united as one, in much the same way that Amanda and her brother Andrew united all creatures when the Light of Compassion blasted through their black little hearts and made them nice. On this sacred day of wholeness, we celebrate *One Light, Many Colors – One Love, Many Creatures.*"

"One Love, Many Creatures," repeats the audience.

"Cherished friends, *let us lift our light and let it shine!*"

The Abahoes pry the illuminum orbs out of their foreheads, raise them high, and slowly sweep them back and forth. Tracking through space, the glow-globes leave luminous trails.

"Sniff!" cries Kika. "Are you seeing this? Everything's in slow motion!"

"Far out," says the dog nibbling glumly at his cape strings.

The drummers slow to a heartbeat. Unusual crystalline harmonies weave into their steady rhythm as the footlights are cloaked to darken the arena.

The audience hushes.

BLASH!

A shard of sunlight explodes through a special crack in the cavern ceiling. It slices through the crystal pillar, blasting rainbows all over the place. Whoops and cheers vibrate through the chamber. The Abahoes' white skin and snowy costumes radiate red, orange, yellow, green, blue, indigo, and violet. "It's a giant prism!" squeals Kika. "Everybody's tie-dyed!"

"Retro," comments Sniff.

Giddy with spirit, Moleems hug Serpenteems. Rateems dance with Gopheems. The clans unite in a riotous outpouring of laughter and love.

Kika twirls wildly. "Look at our colorful capes!"

Sniff's cape has worked its way around his neck so it looks like a bib.

Kika fixes it. "There you go. Snuper-Siff! I mean, Super-Sniff!" Kika gets the giggles.

"Super stupid … and stop laughing," mopes the dog.

She tries, but she can't. Tears roll down her cheeks and her sides ache. She thinks she's going to pee in her shorts but just in time, she sort of pulls it together. "Okay," she gasps. "Okay. Okay. I'm good." The giggles grab her again and she flops to the ground. "Arrgghhhh! Sniff! Help!!"

The dog stares at her blankly, which makes her laugh even harder.

Finally able to catch her breath, Kika manages to sit up. "Sniff," she starts, "Wait … Wait … What was I saying? Oh yeah. Look at my hands. I'm holding a rainbow!"

"I'm color-blind."

"Bummer. Oh no!" she cries. "The colors are all fading away!"

Indeed, as the sun passes by the sacred slot, the chamber dims to dark. The Abahoes cool down and pop the globes back into their glow-holes.

"Is that it?" asks Sniff hopefully. "Can I take this thing off now?"

The drumming cranks up again.

A gathering of Abahoes led by Todd and his maracas, sway to the droning beat and form a circle around the stage. The circle becomes a spiral, which turns into some other geometrical shape. Scrawny arms waving around, their little feet pounding the dirt, they chant in a dull monotone. This goes on for, like, forever.

"Kinda boring," yawns Kika.

"Kind of?" says Sniff.

"I think I'll just rest my eyes for a while."

"Me too."

CHAPTER 13

Kika awakens to an insistent nudging against her ankles and calves. She can barely move. Her neck aches, and her brain feels gluey as oatmeal. She hears the blood thudding in her ears. With effort, she squints open her hot, heavy eyelids. The air is deathly quiet. The Abahoes are gone and the gravel ghosts are back.

Kika swallows, but her throat feels clogged with cotton-balls. In a fog, she manages to sit up. The cavern spins. Fumbling for her headlamp and water bottle, she smells sulfur. *Shoot. Forgot to rinse it out.*

"Sniff?" she says.

No answer.

"Snifferton? Alan?"

Silence. Dread.

Kika scrambles over to where the dog had been sleeping and discovers his soiled cape trampled into the dirt.

Snifferton is gone.

Kika stares in horrid disbelief. She trembles. Her heart races. Shaking her head clear, she takes slow, deep breaths and says to herself, *Kika, you're totally okay. Everything's fine. It's just a mini-meltdown and you're getting through it. Stop freaking yourself out and do what you need to do. You can panic later when you have more time.* Kika rises, grabs her backpack and stuffs it with the bartered food and booty.

The prodding against her legs turns urgent. "Gravel ghosts," she says forcefully, "where's Sniff?" Kika feels nipping at her ankles. She takes a few steps forward. The pinching stops, but the pressure continues. She tries the opposite direction. Pinching.

Okay – So, pinching, wrong direction. Pushing, right direction. Right direction? Really? Should I trust them? Maybe just for now. Snifferton is waiting.

"All right, ghosts!" she says, all bossy. "Let's move!"

The creepy things twisting around her legs, prod her through warm passages and cool tunnels choked with roots. Kika imagines woody arms reaching out to grab her. The air feels thick with spirits. Pockmarked walls morph into ghoulish faces that vanish as she passes. Sticky threads brushing against her skin leave a stinging slime. Clicks and rattles chatter nearby. Dampness soaking through her flimsy T-shirt, Kika trudges on. *Slip-slap, slip-slap* smack her trusty thongs against the soggy earth. Still wondering if she's going in the right direction, Kika remembers the fortuneteller's poem:

If it's not *Yes*, it must be *No*.

Trust your Light. You're good to go.

Shifting her headlamp, Kika rubs between her eyebrows. She thinks hard – harder than she ever thought before. Then she listens even harder.

Plink, plink, plink, plink. The weep of seeping water interrupts her reverie. Dripping stalactites grip the cavern ceiling. Crawling with glowing green centipedes, stalagmites thrust up through the earth like gleaming fangs. Kika squeezes through. Something screeches past her ear, its leathery wings scraping her cheek. Her thighs cramp and blisters swell between her toes. She's desperately thirsty. "Keep going. Find Sniff. You're bigger than this. You're tough. You're tough," she chants in rhythm with her footsteps. The trickling water deepens into a stream and then widens into a river.

Kika freezes. *Is that a cry?* It sounds so faint, she wonders if the creek geeks and stream demons are teasing her.

She hears it again. A cry. A howl. Snifferton's howl!

Kika rushes toward it, but the gravel ghosts resist. They pinch fiercely, trying to lead her in another direction. The baying continues and then a bark echoes through the canyon.

Kika stops. She takes a deep breath, and then asks her Light, "Do I follow the ghosts? Are they leading me to Sniff?" Inside herself she does not feel a *Yes*. The answer, then, is *No!*

Kika strides toward the river – toward Snifferton's howl. The gravel ghosts growl a warning. She tries to shake them off, but they pinch harder. Ignoring the pain, she stumbles forward. The menacing pests sting her calves, their tentacles scalding her flesh.

"Kika, over here!" shriek the creek geeks.

"Jump in! Jump in!" the stream demons scream.

Kika plunges her burning legs into the river. The furious gravel devils hiss and spit as the geeks and demons go to work. Kika struggles to keep her balance while an underwater battle rages around her calves. The churning and splashing finally subside. A putrid wisp of steam rises from the surface, and then vanishes. The ghosts are history.

Kika takes a great lungful of air and surrenders to the cold, wet relief. Once her body has quieted, she fills her bottle, gulps greedily, and wades to shore. She tears into a chunk of potato bread from her pack and follows it with another blissfully long drink. Refreshed, Kika picks her way through the shallows to retrieve a flip-flop that had washed downstream. She thanks the geeks and demons who burble with delight.

The dog's howling has stopped, but Kika now knows the way. Taking the trail along the river, she feels full in her belly, sure in her mind and brave in her heart.

CHAPTER 14

Kika hears it again – Snifferton's wail, louder with every step. She slogs on, sensing curious eyes peering at her behind every boulder.

A yelp, loud and clear, bursts out of a wall of limestone. Kika rushes toward it. Searching along the rocky surface, her fingers find a crack. She rips off her headlamp, turns her face and presses her hot cheek against the cold crag. As her eye scans the dimness, it finds a miserable, panting heap collapsed on the floor of a cramped cell. Exhaustion racks his beautiful body. When he moves, a thick cord tightens around his neck. His paws bleed from trying to dig his way out. He shivers. He whimpers. He waits.

Snifferton.

Kika's face flushes with fury. She chokes back a sob. "Sniff," she whispers through the opening. His soulful suede eyes open, his head lifts, and his velvety nose tests the air. "Kika?"

"I'm here, Sniff."

"Kika," he says, "they hurt me."

"Oh, Sniff. Just hang in there, buddy. I'm going to …"

"Gotcha!"

Kika whirls. Her backpack slams into something big and sweaty and strong. They crash to the ground. Kika scrambles to get up, but the thing is *on* her. In a flash he binds her wrists and yanks her forward.

"Go," he grunts.

Kika falters.

"Go!"

"I am!" she shouts struggling to her feet. "Jerk," she says under her breath.

He snaps the rope.

"Ow. Ow. Ow!" she cries. "I didn't mean …"

"You callin' me *mean*?" he stammers. "Well … um … you're rubber. No, I'm rubber. You're glue. Whatever you say bounces off me and sticks to your head."

"Oh, brother," mutters Kika.

"I'm not yer brother," he says shoving her forward.

"Okay," says Kika. "Don't have a cow."

"What?"

"I said … never mind."

"You better mind," the thing grumbles.

As they lurch through the gloomy canyon, Kika notices a scattering of orange specks flickering out of the rock walls. Closer up, they appear to be small bonfires, like *luminarias* at Christmas. Their light radiates from entrances carved into the cliffs. Through the smoke, Kika catches glimpses of figures scurrying up and down networks of narrow terraces. They pass a gold embossed plaque that reads, WELCOME TO NORTH DARKODA. NOW GO AWAY. Distracted, Kika rams into the fat, hairy back of her captor.

"Gross!" she yelps.

"Go in," he snorts, pushing her through a low doorway.

Unsteady, Kika gropes along a corridor stinking of decay. Close behind, the troll huffs and shuffles, his oniony breath hot on the back of her neck. The moldy path leads through dank passageways until it spits them out into a great chamber. Its stale air barely feeds a circle of sputtering candles. Covering the walls, Kika notes the same strange symbols she had seen before; only these are inlayed with thick gold leaf. The hazy room glimmers dimly.

A pebble clatters to the floor. Peering through the shifting gloom, Kika sees someone – or some thing – staring down at her from a high stone balcony.

CHAPTER 15

"Yo," blurts the shadow from the terrace.

Kika glowers.

The figure bounds gracefully and lands in front of her, puffing lightly and smelling goaty. He isn't all that bad looking, if you don't count the unibrow, nose hairs and missing left eye. He's also naked, except for a knee-length skort, black dress socks covering his bushy calves and itty-bitty pointy slippers on his itty-bitty pointy feet. A gaudy crown perches precariously upon two lumps that he tries to hide with an elaborate pumpkin-colored comb-over. He sticks out his hairy knuckles. "Fist bump," he says, and then notices Kika's hands are still tied.

"Ooops. Light's not great in here." He kneels down and nibbles her free.

"I'm MaaajesT," he slurs through a mouthful of rope, which he chews and swallows. "You might have heard of me. Troll King? Hey, cute hair. Do you use product? And, by the way, Kiki, what took you so long? I told the G-ghosts to get you here ASAP."

"My name is Kika," she snaps, all business. "Now let him go."

MajesT casually digs a strand of fiber out of his gums with a grimy thumbnail.

"Didn't you hear me?" says Kika with attitude. "I said, let him go."

"Who?" he replies, inspecting his teeth in some sort of shiny oval thing hanging from a heavy gold chain around his scabby neck.

"My dog!" yells Kika.

"Oh my goodness. Indoor voice. Please!"

If Kika had been her boring little eleven-year-old self, she never would have had the guts to stand up to this sleazoid. "I want my dog back, now!"

"Ooh I'm so scared," he says, and then, "He's safe. Let's have the stuff."

"What stuff?"

"Hello – the ransom? For your *pooch*?"

A blip of spit spritzes Kika's T-shirt.

"Say it, don't spray it," mentions Brad from his corner.

"Open your pack," says MajesT. "Pretty please?" In an awful singsongy voice he continues, "I know what's in there. Illuminum goodies. We saw them when we nabbed him."

"Why didn't you just take them then, and leave us alone?"

"And leave us alone," he mimics.

"Why did you have to kidnap him?"

"No gift, no glow, no go," he answers with a big fake smile.

"What are you talking about?"

The troll wrenches the pack away from Kika and rifles through it until he finds an illuminum bracelet. In his hand, it looks tarnished and dull. In Kika's, the luster returns and it glistens like a star. When she gifts it to him, it stays sparkly. He

129

caresses the jewel with reverence and purrs, "Its light is precious to us here in North Darkoda, and it's also pretty."

"So," begins Kika, "you're saying that I have to give my treasure to you as a gift, otherwise it loses its light?"

"'Fraid so," MajesT replies, checking himself out in his medallion for, like the millionth time.

"And, if I do," she continues, "you'll let my dog go. Right?"

"Yes, of course. Of course," he sighs, a sneaky glint in his yellow eyes – eye.

"Okay. Fine. But I'm not handing over the goods until the prisoner is delivered." Kika remembers this from a thriller she'd just seen on HBO.

"Okay. Okay. Sheesh," the troll says, all inconvenienced. "Bradley! Fetch the flea-bitten cur!"

"Huh?" replies the galoot, investigating a gob of earwax.

"The *d o g*," enunciates his boss.

"Oh," responds Brad dully. "All right." He

trips and lumbers off.

"And hurry up!" shouts Kika surprising her-self in a good way.

"Whoa," says MajesT. "Feisty. I like that in my mortals. I know! Let's sit down and have a chat while we wait, kay? Heard any good dirt?"

Kika senses movement over her shoulder. Four impish children sneak out of the shadows. They look exactly like MajesT, only tinier. Some wear diapers, some don't.

"Josh? Jeremy? Jason? Jolene?" goo goos their father in a hideous baby voice. "Come over here and greet our guest."

They toddle forward. Through the gloom, their straw-colored eyes glisten like shiny brass buttons. One reaches up its hairy little arms to Kika and begs to be held. Two others climb into her lap. The fourth teethes on her thong. Under their breath, they make a *maaing* sound.

"They want you to sing them a song," says the troll.

"Um," says Kika, totally creeped out.

"Okay, okay," he says. "Didn't mean to put

you on the spot. I have one. Gather 'round Papa. No butting!" In an alarming falsetto, he trills,

"Four little lambikins dancing on a cliff.
One kicked the other over.
Piff. Piff. Piff.
Three little lambikins splashing in the stream.
One drowned the other one.
Scream. Scream. Scream.
Two little lambikins eating barley stew.
One poisoned the other one.
Boo hoo hoo.
One little lambikin near the fire pit.
He tripped and tumbled in.
And then that was it."

The little ones shriek in merriment. "Again! Again! Again!" they bleat, clambering all over Kika.

"All right, you nubbins. Simmer down. Auntie Kiki doesn't like children."

"Ouch! It's not that …"

"No problemo." He shoos them away. "Go

on, little chops. Go play on the rock pile, or someplace else."

As they crawl back into wherever, Kika notices a small yellow puddle on the floor.

MajesT smiles and shakes his knobby noggin. "Kids," he says sheepishly. "You keep staring at my neckpiece, Kiki. Are you admiring my medallion?"

"Uh. No. Your chain." Kika clears her throat. "The gold?"

"Oh, we find chunks of this junk all over the place. But, it's easy to work with, and it gives our graffiti some class." He fingers his medallion. "Now *this* is valuable. One-of-a-kind. It's called a Maybelline." Kika stares at him in puzzlement. "See?" he says, "It's written right here." The troll points to words printed on a small plastic makeup mirror. Kika doesn't dare mention that her mother has the exact same one in her purse. "Um, nice," she says.

"Extraordinary! My very own little reflecting pool. Boo-Boo-Boo, I love youuu," he oozes, kissing his reflection. "My Maybelline."

133

Kika glances anxiously toward the doorway. *What's taking them so long?*

"So, Kiki …"

"Kika."

"Kikaaaa – do you like what I'm wearing?"

Whaaaat?

"I guess," she replies, not caring at *all.*

MajesT reaches into the backpack, grabs a large illuminum brooch, and pins it to his skort. "Better? Or a little much? I don't want to over-accessorize." He snatches a ring. "Does this make my pinkie look fat? Ooooh." He yanks out Kika's headlamp. "This looks promising." He frees his crown and slams the lamp over his greasy mullet. The unfortunate lumps on his forehead cause a problem – two problems. "Ah, well," he laments, peeling it off and handing it back. "Nice. But, not really *me.*"

A thunderous bark bounces off the cavern walls. MajesT claps his hands over his ears. "Yipes."

"Sniff!" cries Kika. She rushes to her scruffy pal. His tail whisks the smoky air into a billow.

He wriggles around in his happy puppy dance, then rises up and plops his paws on Kika's shoulders. She giggles and scrunches up her face as he licks her nose and eyelids and cheeks.

"Ugh," says the troll, turning away in disgust. "Get a room."

He whirls back and growls, "The hand-off. Now." His eye glints in greedy anticipation.

Kika dumps the remaining contents of her backpack onto the ground and separates out the jewelry. MajesT dabs a bubble of drool off his skeevy goatee. "Bradley, my man, be our witness." The goon, caught with his finger up his nose, snorts.

"Okay, Kiki," MajesT pants, "gather up the loot, my lambikin."

She pulls it into her lap.

"Goody. Now, repeat after me, I Kiki …"

"I Kika,"

"Do hereby willingly and *lovingly* …" the creature flutters his eye coyly.

"Do hereby, willingly and (gag) lovingly …"

"Gift all my illuminum treasure to my new

135

BFF, MajesT the Extremely Magnificent."

"Gift all my illuminum treasure to my new BFFMajesTtheExtremelyMagnificent."

"Now, shove it over to Daddy. Happy birthday to me. Happy birthday to me. *M m m m m m m*," hums the troll, pawing the plunder.

Kika stuffs everything else back into her pack and grabs Sniff. Brad blocks their way.

"More, pretty please," coos the king.

"What?" starts Kika. "You said …"

"More!" he croaks. "You have an *in* with those Abahoe twerps. Go back downriver and get me more!"

"How?" protests Kika, so over it.

"Um … swim? Ha ha. Just kidding. No, we'll lend you a raft. Buuuuuttttt, to make sure you come back, you must leave me your most prized possession – just like in fairy tales. And I don't mean the dog. That horrific howling aggravated my rash. What else you got in that bag, Kiki?"

Kika thinks fast. She rifles through her pack. "My mystical Disneyland sweatshirt?"

"Eek, a mouse. I'll pass."

"Gluten-free root ragout?" she offers. "Organic potato bread?"

"Eww."

"Tutu?"

"I'm tempted."

"The only thing left," cries Kika piteously, "is something I can't possibly part with. I've had it since I was a Brownie. It means everything to me. Please don't make me give it to you. Pretty please – with sugar on it?"

"Well, if you love it so much, why don't you marry it?"

Brad guffaws. "Good one."

MajesT snaps his grubby fingers. "Gimme."

Kika reaches into her pack and, with great ceremony, presents her Girl Scout flashlight. The smarmball lunges for it.

"Careful," says Kika, clutching it close. "It's fragile and, um, one-of-a-kind."

Sniff rolls his eyes.

"What does it do?" MajesT wheezes.

"It gives," Kika pauses for dramatic effect, "Light … lots and lots of light. Just push this magic button and you have light! Way brighter than illuminum."

"Lemme see. Lemme see." Kika taps the switch and hands it to him. A silvery beam pierces through the gloom. "Oh my," he whispers.

"And look," says Kika, prying it out of his clammy grip. "You can write your name with it."

"Me likee!" he squeals.

Kika continues, "Check out what happens when I do this." She shines the flashlight up under MajesT's giant chin. He peers into his Maybelline. "Ooooh. Spooky face. I'll take it."

"No!" pleads Kika. "No! Please! No! Okay."

"Might as well throw in the tutu too."

"Tutu too. Heh heh," chortles Brad.

"Anyway, you know the drill – I, Kiki "

"I, Kika …"

"Kika, Kookoo, Kaka … Do hereby … blah di blah, blah, blah – this flashlight … blah di blah … MajesT the Extremely Magnificent. Bradley, my man, did you get all that?"

Bradley farts.

"Good enough. Please escort them to the river. Be back soon, kiddies – *very* soon. Love ya. Miss ya."

Following Brad, Kika helps a limping Sniff down a stone ramp to the water's edge. The raft is a contraption of logs and reeds sloppily tethered together with fraying rope. Once boarded, the troll hands Kika a pair of mismatched oars and pushes them away from shore.

He waves, "See you. Wouldn't wanna be you – I mean *me* – no … hmmm. " Scratching his head, he clumps back up the ramp to watch Ma-jesT play space ninja with his new toy.

CHAPTER 16

"**B**rilliant job, Kika. Saved our butts," says Sniff, nursing his sore paws. "I can't believe how fierce you were."

"I know. It was weird. At first, I just pretended to be brave, but after awhile, I really felt brave."

Taking a break from his feet, Sniff asks, "Kika, where are we going – really."

Kika shrugs her shoulders. "I have no idea. That's why it's called an …"

"Adventure."

They sigh.

The two sit in silence for a long time – Sniff licking, water lapping. North Darkoda's *luminarias* twinkle out, and darkness returns. The raft makes a gentle, creaking sound.

To relieve her blisters, Kika takes off her thongs and stows them in the backpack. Resting her head on her dog's warm belly, her mind wanders. She daydreams about Chev and how awesome it was that he asked for her number and how did Mr. Wiggley tie that sheet into yoga pants and what is the meaning of existence and …

Sniff wonders what's for lunch.

In the midst of her imaginings, Kika has the vague feeling that she and Sniff are now in the bed of an old mining car lazily cruising down a smooth road.

"Earth to Kika," nudges Sniff.

"What?" she says, checking back in. Kika is intrigued to find herself in the bed of an old mining car lazily cruising down a smooth road. She looks back to see their raft wedged in a sandbar, getting smaller and smaller, then disappearing altogether in a swirling grey fog.

"How did we …"

"Kika," laughs Sniff, "you don't remember this car picking us up when the raft got stuck?"

"Um …" she replies. "Kind of."

"Brain fog," states Sniff. "Well, you were definitely somewhere else."

So many peculiar things have happened to Kika recently that she looks upon this latest development with curiosity rather than alarm.

Driverless, the little car seems to know its way, or maybe it's on rails. It moves slower and slower until it runs out of track.

Kika and Sniff hardly exit the vehicle when a person with a very large head crashes into them. He's bent over in a C shape, and he has no mouth. In his hands he holds a globe of the world. Texting furiously on it, his thumbs are a blur. Other beings materialize out of the mist, colliding with each other, changing directions, and stopping unexpectedly. Their bowed backs make it impossible for them to look anywhere but down.

In the midst of this chaos stands a little island of calm – a poppy-red pagoda with a pointed golden roof. The scroll above the open entrance reads: THIS WAY IN – THIS WAY OUT. Inside, a holy man in a lavender tank top and drawstring pants sits on a stack of cushions, meditating. Unlike the others, he's a perfectly normal-looking guru guy with a man-bun, beard, and mouth.

The two approach. Unsure of how to address him, Kika tries, "Excuse me, uh, Mr. Awareness?"

He opens his eyes, places his palms together, and bows, "Ommar, please."

Kika bows back. Sniff stretches into Downward-Facing Dog.

"Would you like a cup of tepid jasmine tea?"

"Yes, please," says Kika.

"I'll just take a bone if you have one," says Sniff.

"Sorry," Ommar sighs, "Vegetarian. But I can offer you this delightful bulgur bar."

"That sounds delicious," says Sniff, having no idea.

Kat Sawyer

The three gather around a low, lacquered table. A faint scent of patchouli emanates from his eminence.

"Ommar," says Kika. "Where are we?"

"You are here now," he replies, his voice all spiritual.

"Okaaay," starts Kika, "but where is Herenow?"

"It's not there then."

Kika tries another approach. "Umm. So, we were driven here?"

"Yes," he answers.

"Where were we driven?"

"To Distraxion."

"But why? How?"

"Oh, there are many ways to get here," he says smiling serenely. "Daydreaming, musing, zoning out, not listening, fantasizing, staring into space, going unconscious, losing focus, spacing out, or simply not paying attention."

"Oh," nods Kika, wishing she had sugar for her tea. "And how do we get out of Distraxion?"

"By doing the opposite."

144

"I see," says Kika, not seeing at all.

"A question," says Sniff who had been quietly taking it all in, including the bulgur bar. "Who are those others?"

"They are the Savvies. Their minds and bodies are enslaved by the Almighty Tek."

He explains how Tek put the whole world into the hands of the Savvies, but, because they converse solely through their thumbs, they have lost the power of speech – not to mention, lips. They can't see each other because their backbones will not allow them to stand up straight, and, since they live only in their minds, their heads are very big. The Savvies remain unknowingly trapped in Tek's web, for they have traded communion for communication. Ommar finishes with, "Falsely believing they are connecting, they remain alone."

"Aren't they lonely?" asks Kika.

"Not really. They're so busy in Distraxion that they don't think about being lonely – except when they do – and then, they seek entertainment."

"Oh," says Kika, still a little fuzzy about the whole thing. She considers asking the monk more about Tek, but is afraid it could lead to a new Adventure, and she really wants to be home before dinner.

"So, Ommar," begins Sniff. "Why are you here?"

"Well, when Savvies feel overwhelmed, confused, or achingly lonely, they come to me and I liberate them from Tek."

"How?" asks Kika.

"I teach them the practice of Now. Nowism. The Savvies' spines straighten, speech returns, and they can once again look into each other's eyes. They have learned to be here, now – not in Distraxion."

"But, if they're here now, how can they not be in Distraxion?" asks Kika, totally befuddled.

"Yes."

Whaaaaaattt?

"Ommar," says Sniff, taking over, "we don't really want to be here now."

"Ahh, that is the problem my dear dog. Few

do. They would rather live in Distraxion. It's easier – and more amusing."

"So," says Sniff. "The only way to get out of Distraxion is to *be here now*."

"Precisely," he replies.

"Then," continues Sniff, "*be here now* simply means paying attention to what you're doing while you're doing it. Wherever you are. And to get out of Distraxion, you have to focus every step of the way and …"

"… eventually," continues the monk, "you'll be somewhere else experiencing here and now where you are then. That is the Way of the Now."

This all makes Kika's head hurt, but she's willing to try anything to get back to the raft.

"Ommar," she starts, "I'm not sure if I …"

"Perhaps," he says, reading her mind or something, "a verse will make this more under-standable."

Twiddling his prayer beads, he begins,

"Yesterday's gone. Tomorrow will be.
The Present's all that's real, you see.

147

Clear your mind. Don't let it stray.
Love what's going on today.
Here and now is where it's at.
Nothin' you can do 'bout that,
except enjoy each perfect minute.
Live your life while you are in it."

Ommar rises and leads the two outside. Bowing, he backs away into the fog. "Stay on track, seekers. Enjoy the journey."

"Sniff …" starts Kika.

"Don't worry, I got this. Watch me." With perfect concentration, Sniff puts one paw in front of the other, then the other and the other and the other. Kika does the same, only with two – feet, not paws. Duh.

Slowly and mindfully she and Sniff make their way alongside the rails leading from Distraxion to the river. When Kika's brain wanders, so does her body. She often finds herself in a ditch; but the more she focuses, the easier it is to remain on the path. By walking this way, Kika is surprised to discover many wonderful things: the comforting squish of sand between her toes, pale curly moss adorning lovely-shaped boulders, colorful pebbles, a slight salty breeze brushing her skin and the deep earthy smell of the land. She hears the river quite clearly. Her shoulders drop and she relaxes into the moment. The fog clears.

"Hey Sniff," she says, "Way of the Now is cool. I never noticed so much around me before. How did you learn to do this?"

"I used to be a yoga teacher … not really. It comes naturally to animals. We pretty much live in the moment all the time."

"So, Sniff," starts Kika, "do I think too much about what happened yesterday and what's going to happen tomorrow? Do I spend too much time in Distraxion?"

"Maybe a little," replies the dog tactfully. "But most humans do."

"Well, I'm going to practice Nowism from now on – wherever I am – if I can remember. I don't want to miss out on stuff. Plus, when I'm really doing what I'm doing while I'm doing it, I'm not stressed."

… for the first time in her life.

"Sniff!" she cries. "I can't believe we're here already! There's our raft. And it's not stuck anymore."

The two hop on and shove away from shore.

Rowing downstream, Kika smiles as she enjoys the simple, soothing *plish* of her oar as it swooshes through the water.

C H A P T E R   1 7

B^{OOM!}

Startled, Kika looks up. "Sniff," she says pointing, "Over there. Are those fireworks?" Through the dark, explosions flash and voices thunder. Kika and Sniff carefully approach what looks like a battle zone. They tuck into the shore to watch in safety. Two extremely tall figures on either bank fire what look like grenades at each other across the river. The missiles burst in sparkles and sentences.

"Those look like the Triten twins," whispers

Sniff. "Clee and Shay."

"How did you ..." starts Kika.

"I saw the biopic."

So, imagine an attractive giant dressed cap to boots in camo, frowning. Now, double it and you have the Tritens. Their pinched faces and clenched jaws show the seriousness of their verbal assaults. They each stand behind a heap of ammo, stubby launchers pressed against their shoulders.

"What are they doing?" asks Kika.

"Hurling insults," replies Sniff.

Clee, or maybe Shay, aims and shoots.

YOU'RE NUTTY AS A FRUITCAKE explodes the put-down in a spangle of stars. It doesn't appear to be anywhere near its intended target, but it does make a lot of noise.

The other giant launches, YOU'RE THIN AS A RAIL!

Word bombs burst through the air in alarming succession.

YOU EAT LIKE A PIG!

YOU'RE SLOW AS A SNAIL!

YOU'RE STUBBORN AS A MULE!

YOU'RE CLUMSY AS AN OX!

YOU'RE DUMB AS DIRT!

YOU'RE DUMB AS ROCKS!

When the twins lob at the same time, the explosion sounds something like, YOU BIG STINK AS A SKUNK HOUSE!

Having heard enough, Kika and Sniff crouch down, and while the Tritens pause to reload, they quickly paddle away unnoticed.

Looking over her shoulder, she says, "Man, that was …"

"Insulting," says Sniff.

"Well, they weren't very original," says Kika, "and since they're twins, aren't they really putting themselves down?"

"Yep," says Sniff. "That's how it works."

"So," continues Kika, "when you judge someone, you're really judging something in yourself that you don't like, to make yourself feel better, but you both end up …"

"… feeling bad," finishes the dog.

"Wow," says Kika looking troubled. "So if a person judges herself for her bad hair or her big feet or saying dorky things, she might turn out to be like the Tritens?"

"Maybe," says Sniff. "So to be safe, it's always best for a person like that to love herself for exactly who she is."

"Oh."

Kika paddles and ponders and paddles and ponders. *So many lessons. I guess life is the homework – and the spelling test.*

CHAPTER 18

"I'm thirsty as a desert," says Sniff dryly.

"Um ..." starts Kika, "we're kind of surrounded by water here? Just put your lips together and lap."

Sniff shifts around until his head dangles over the side.

Thump.

"Easy, boy."

"Wasn't me."

Bump!

A stronger shove rocks the raft. "Sniff," says

Kika. "Pull your head back."

From the water's inky surface rises a menacing entity. Then others, too many to count. Slick and snaky, they rear their evil heads out of their liquid lair. "River vipers!" shouts Kika.

Sniff snaps at the wriggling monsters. Balancing unsteadily, Kika yells and swings at them with her oar. Making contact, it shatters. The smaller snakes, frightened off, dive and disappear. The largest recoils but glides back angrily and circles.

"Paddle!" shouts Kika.

"I can't!" yelps Sniff. "I don't have opposable thumbs!"

"Dogs paddle! Sniff, try to paddle with your paws!"

Sniff lies belly-down on the raft like it's a surfboard, but his front legs don't reach the water. "This is awkward," he whines.

"Then just hold on!" Kika grabs the other oar and pulls furiously.

A pale, dripping mouth gleams in the gloom, its sinister hiss cutting through the roar of the roil-

157

ing river. As the craft jolts, the bow springs up with Sniff clutching desperately. Kika topples into the river. Her fingers let go of the oar as she grabs onto the slippery ropes. A cold tube of muscle slithers along her bare legs. She screams. With all her strength, she heaves herself back on board. The timbers shiver. Kika feels the tethers slacken and the craft waver.

They pick up speed.

"Rapids!" yells Kika. "We're aiming straight into them. I think we can lose the viper there!"

Wicked whitecaps pummel their bodies and send clouds of spray exploding against the jutting boulders.

Gripping with bleeding claws, Sniff wails. Kika glues her body to his back and clings to the sides of the raft. Rocks scrape its underbelly. Breakers pound. Bouncing and twisting, the two hurtle through the dark canyon.

Suddenly, all before them is empty space.

"No no no no!" shrieks Kika. "Waterfall!"

The raft noses to the edge. Its back lifts, and over the cascade they plummet, spinning and tumbling in the surging curtain of water. They hit the lower pool where the pressure of the falls pushes them under. Lungs bursting, they bob to the surface, still miraculously attached to the raft. Sniff moans. Kika holds him tight.

The tumult subsides and all goes eerily still. The raft groans ominously.

Relieved that the river has quieted, Kika eases herself off her quivering companion. "Sniff?"

He struggles to a sit and stammers, "S-s-sorry about the p-paddling, Kika."

"Oh, Sniff. You did fine." She so wants to hug him but fears that any sudden movement could put them in jeopardy.

The craft makes a lazy circle. As if summoning its strength, the spiral tightens. The raft shimmies. Water seeps through widening gaps in its loosened logs. With a sickening smack, the ropes let go, scattering timber like pick-up sticks. The fiercely swirling water carries Sniff away. Kika sees the whites of his terrified eyes and his dark form thrashing to stay afloat. "Sniff, I'm coming!"

Fighting to reach him, her arms dig into the foaming torrent and her legs kick ferociously. A fist of water punches her in the face. Disoriented and exhausted, she's swept into the vortex.

Round and round the girl and dog spin, helpless as sparrows in a storm. Gasping for breath, the cruel river tugs at their pitiful bodies. Again and again they claw to the surface, only to be sucked under. They are too weak, the whirlpool too strong.

They sink.

CHAPTER 19

Kika coughs up a fountain of stream. Her bleary eyes spot her backpack tossed onto the sandy shore. Through water-clogged ears, she hears a whimper and then a hot, sloppy tongue licks her cold, wet face.

"Sniff," she smiles. She buries her face in his soggy dogginess.

When her ears clear, and her breath quiets, she hears a low humming nearby. *That tune! How can that be?* It's the lullaby Mami sang to her when she was a baby.

As Kika's vision sharpens, she beholds a

graceful figure silhouetted against light glowing from the mouth of the cave. Thin as a skeleton, and wearing a dirty white gown, torn and tattered by time, the woman sways in rhythm with her song. Her ratty slippers hover a few feet off the ground.

"Who's that?" whispers Sniff.

"Oh, no. It's Maria – La Llorona. A long time ago, she drowned her two sons in the river to spite her cheating husband. Crazy with grief, she haunts the *acequias* crying and searching for them."

Now, it's not clear how La Llorona, the Weeping Woman of Hispanic legend snuck in here but, New Mexico *is* the Land of Enchantment, so let's just leave it at that.

"Ay! Mis niños!"

"Uh oh," whispers Kika, fastening the backpack and slipping on her thongs. "She thinks we're her kids."

"What?" says Sniff. "Is she blind?"

"I guess all that crying really messed up her eyes. We gotta get outta here. Go, go, go!"

They scramble to their feet, but Maria is nasty fast. She swoops down and hugs them with arms like pincers. *"Pobrecitos,"* she coos, her breath stinking of crawdads and marsh weeds; her teary eyes the color of pond scum. "My poor little ones. I have been searching for you for so long. *Que milagro!* What a miracle it is that the river brought you back to me." She grips Sniff in a neck lock. *"Niñito!"* she cries. *"Mas pequeño* than I remember. But you were always small for your age. And *tanto pelo*! I just don't remember so much hair!"

Sniff winces, but muzzles a nip.

Maria reaches her bony arm around Kika and ruffles her pixie. "And you, *mijo."* She pokes the backpack. *"Tan gordo.* So fat you are, my son – and so lumpy! *No te preocupes.* It doesn't matter. I have found you at last. *Mis lágrimas* are tears of joy." Her face darkens and turns ugly – like a maggoty corpse. "And I will never let you go." She tightens her grip, *"Nunca."*

Sniff twitches, restraining himself from inflicting bodily harm.

"Ay, you're shivering, little one. *Ven. Vengan*

conmigo. Let us all walk out into the sun to-gether."

With supernatural strength, Maria hoists them off their feet. Kika glances over at Sniff whose arms stick out stiffly like table legs. Sniff prefers to have all paws on the ground at all times. He whines softly.

"Oh, little bird," cries the crone, "we're almost there."

The three glide to the mouth of the cave. Through the opening, Kika squints at the most glorious sight – her land, her sky, her magnificent thunderheads blossoming into a late summer storm. A breath catches in her chest. Hot tears prickle behind her eyes – *Home.*

The creature floats her *children* through a dense cottonwood grove to a glade choked with brambles. She settles them on a bench in front of a hut made of sticks and reeds, her hairy arms draped over their shoulders.

The wind grows restless. Turquoise skies turn indigo, and then to slate. The heavens growl.

Rubbing Sniff roughly, La Llorona murmurs,

"Mejor, no? Better, yes? You'll warm up soon."

Kika clears her throat. Sniff catches her eye as she nods toward the backpack. Sniff blinks in acknowledgement.

A splinter of lightening rips open the sky, followed by a smack of thunder. Kika flinches.

"Ay, don't be afraid, *pajarito.*"

Maria tightens her hold on her *son* (Kika plus backpack).

Stifling a gag, Kika cuddles closer to the sickening hag. "Mami," she chokes, "how wonderful it is that we are all together again. We missed you *también.*"

Sniff nestles his head into her disgusting lap.

Kika sings Abuelita's lullaby accompanied by the sky's deep harmony.

"Little birds, don't fly away.
In your mami's *nido* stay ..."

Maria's grip loosens and her head falls back. Her gaping mouth reveals a black tongue and brown molars. She sleep-snorts.

Kika continues, carefully loosening the back-pack straps.

"Safe within your mami's nest."

La Llorona jerks.

Kika freezes. Maria exhales. So do Sniff and Kika.

"Pajaritos, take your rest."

Kika eases her shoulders free. She waits for the next belt of thunder. When it comes, she slips out her arms and bolts.

The creature's head whips up. Sniff snarls a warning, and then bites into her warty wrist. A blue-white flash ignites her furious face, now contorted in a mask of pain. Blinded, she shrieks and lunges for Sniff. He dodges. Raising her shriveled arms, she screeches, *"No son mis hijos!* You're not my sons! Who are you? Answer me! *Quiénes son?"*

An explosion of thunder answers.

"Diablitos! You filthy little devils will not escape. I will find you – or you will find me – in your nightmares!"

The monsoon lets loose its fury. Kika darts through the downpour. Hail like bullets, pelts her body. Her feet skid and slog through the oozing underbrush. Willow limbs slice her skin. The  phantom's ranting grows closer. A sizzle of lightning splits the trunk of a nearby cottonwood. Kika lowers her head and charges forward. She glances over her shoulder to catch the witch's black form soaring and swooping, her fleshless arms flailing, her grotesque skull-face grinning in a horrific howl. Kika trips and goes down. She curls into a ball, shuts her eyes, and freezes. An icy gust, stinking of rot, shoots into her body. Kika feels a rush of sadness, longing, loneliness, and regret as Maria's spirit passes through her.

With one last heart-wrenching wail, La Llorona's misery explodes across the wind-whipped woods and is swallowed by the whining gale.

CHAPTER 20

The exhausted storm lets out one last weary grumble.

Cautiously, Kika straightens her body and staggers to her feet.

"Sniff!" she calls. "Snifferton!" She desperately hopes he escaped.

With bruised ankles, cramping sides, and arms bleeding with scratches, Kika follows the flooded *acequia* that leads to the road.

Hail-shredded leaves whisper as a late afternoon sun peeks from beneath the skirt of a glowing thunderhead. Arching across the silvery heavens, a double rainbow welcomes Kika home.

"Sniff!" she calls again, scanning the road for her friend. She crawls up a grassy bank for a better view.

An early cricket chirrups out of a nearby chamisa bush. Coyotes trill from the hilltops. Then, the best sound of all excites Kika's ears. Panting. Panting. Snifferton Woolypad's panting! He bounds up the hill behind her. Kika leaps to greet her happy, soppy pup. They wrestle and tussle and crumple into a blissful heap.

Taking a giant belly breath, Kika stretches out onto the cool, wet grass to gaze at plushy cloud characters frisking overhead. *There's a rabbit and a serpent, two giants, and four goaty-looking little blobs.* A wave of wonder washes over her as she remembers the Belowlands – where she was then and who she is now. Kika sits up and shakes her head in amazement.

"Wow, Sniff, Wow!"

Sniff's tail pounds a puddle.

Kika smiles, "Well, *that* wasn't boring."

The dog's wide mouth stretches into a

gigantic grin.

Kika pets the little white patch on his chest as they watch the sky turn pink and then to tangerine.

"Okay, buddy," she sighs. "I guess we'd better get going or I'll be grounded for like a zillion years."

The travelers shuffle down the storm-drenched road.

Weird, thinks Kika. *Why do my flip-flops sound so loud?*

No cricket chirps.

No singing dogs yip.

Sundown holds its breath.

"Catalina!"

"Uh-oh," says Kika. "It's Mami."

Sniff's ears drop and his tail tucks between his legs.

"Kika!"

"Mami." says Kika. "I'm right here, Mami. Wake up."

Mami's lashes part to see the dear, worried face of her daughter and the shiny wet nose of Snifferton Woolypads at her bedside.

"Kika," she whispers, her eyes brimming.

"Mami," sniffles Kika, "Don't cry. I'm sorry I let the screen door slam. I didn't mean …"

"Shhh, Catalina. It's okay." She sits up and takes Kika's hand. "*Mis lágrimas* are tears of joy. And don't worry about the door, *mija*. I went right back to sleep. I had the most wonderful dream."

She pats the mattress playfully. "Come lie here next to me. Alan too, okay?" The dog's ears perk.

"Alan?" asks Kika.

"Sí," Mami giggles. "That was his name in my dream."

Whoa. Kika had never seen her mother so fun and laid-back and Sniff wasn't ever allowed on the bed. They scrunch down into the crispy cool pillows. Her mother strokes her daughter's forehead. *"Ay, mija,* you're so hot and sweaty."

"We just got back from the Romeros," says

Kika. "I found Sniff out there playing Frisbee with the cousins, so I hung with Todd and Pammi for a while."

"Ah," Mami says with a funny look on her face. She runs her fingers through Kika's damp curls. "Do you think we should let your hair grow out?"

Whaaaaat?

"Umm, yes," Kika replies, "I really really think we should."

"Bueno. Now where were we?"

"Your dream?"

"Sí. Well, there was a horrible troll and a funny musician and three evil mermaids. And," she says, making an icky face, "People ate gr-rrrrubbbbs!" She tickles Kika 'til she squeals.

Mami laughs, "There was a crazy circus in a crystal cave and a wicked whirlpool ..." She pets the dog's silky back. "And Alan talked. He was very smart."

Sniff's tail thumps the blanket.

"I wish he could teach me long division, " says Kika.

"I'm sure he could. And guess what?"

"What?"

"It all happened *under the ground.*"

"Wow" says Kika. "Sounds spooky but neat. I wish I was there."

"You were," says her mother.

"Seriously?"

"*Sí,* Kika. I was dreaming about *you.*"

"Whoa." Kika plans to get details later, but right now she's enjoying every precious second of snuggling with her happy mother and awesome dog. A late morning breeze rustles through the sweet olive tree outside their window. Lavender leaf shadows shimmy on the bedroom walls.

"Kika?" Mami asks softly, "Do you know what I'm dreaming about now?"

"What," she says trying to guess in her mind.

"Green chile cheeseburgers!"

"Oh!" cries Kika. "And shakes?"

"*Por supuesto.* Of course. What flavor for you, *mija?*"

"I don't know."

"Not an answer."

"Umm," thinks Kika, "Strawberry?"

"Is that a question?"

"Strawberry!"

"Muy bien!" claps Mami. "And then a whole day together – just you and me – with many more to come." She hugs her daughter. *"Te amo, mija.* So much."

"I love you, too, Mami. So much."

Her mother stares deeply into her daughter's eyes. "Kika," she says, "are you ready?"

Kika stutters, "Ready for … what?"

"Ay, don't be frightened, little bird. Be brave, okay?"

"Okay."

"And," continues Mami, "Let's not *wait* … ever again. *Now* is all we have, yes?"

"I guess," replies Kika, "Yeah."

"So I ask you once more," her mother says, twinkling with mischief. "Are you ready?"

"Yes," laughs Kika, loving this, "I'm ready."

"All right, then, beautiful daughter. Let's go do an Adventure!"

Dear Reader,

If you think this book was cool, please leave
us a review on Amazon!

Thanks a bunch!

Love,
Kika and Sniff

About the Author

A native Californian with a lively imagination, Kat Sawyer's passion is for the visual, written, and performed arts.

She boasts over four decades of television, film and voice-over credits. With a goofy sense of humor and strong connection to her inner kid, Kat has delighted in her work with young people. She was a TV commercial acting coach, a theater mentor for youth in juvenile detention, and has two scene books for kids and teens available through Samuel French.

Moving to glorious New Mexico profoundly inspired Sawyer's award-winning landscape paintings and her practice as a yoga teacher. Her *Voices from the Mat – Yoga Poems and Meditations* was the Grand Prize Winner: Poetry in the 2015 Kindle Book Promos Book Contest.

Kat's essays have appeared in *Cosmopolitan*, *The Artists' Magazine*, *Westways*, *The Artists' Sketchbook*, and *Ms Fitness*. Her poetry is featured in the *Suisun Valley Review*, *Lummox Anthology*, and *Weaving the Terrain: Poetry of the American Southwest*.

In Santa Fe, Kat shares her life with patient husband, JP and spirit-dog, Bill.

About the Illustrator

Brandon McKinney is a storyboard artist for television animation, a comic book artist and children's book illustrator. He's worked for Warner Bros., Hasbro Animation, Marvel Animation, Warp Graphics, Darby Pop Comics, Dark Horse Comics, Electronic Arts and Lucasfilm, among many other companies over his thirty-year career.

Growing up, Brandon became enthralled by Spider-Man comics and the Star Wars films. Those propelled his desire to tell stories with pictures, and he started drawing every day. He got his first job in comics while he was still in high school. He went on to earn his B.A. in Fine Art at UCLA, which helped launch a new chapter in Brandon's career working as a storyboard artist.

Brandon was raised in California, and after living in Florida for over a decade, has returned to the Golden State. He is the father of four incredible kids who watch a few of the cartoons he's worked on.

ALSO BY KAT SAWYER

Voices from the Mat – Yoga Poems and
Meditations (Amazon)

Contemporary Scenes for Contemporary Kids
(Samuel French)

Minute Monologues for Contemporary Teens
(Samuel French)

Made in the USA
San Bernardino, CA
12 December 2019

61347684R00104